GEORGE MACBETH

THE SAMURAI

Harcourt

Brace

Jovanovich

New York

and London

Printed in the United States of America

Library of Congress Cataloging in Publication Data

MacBeth, George.
 The samurai.

 I. Title.
PZ4.M1184Sam3   [PR6063.A13]   823'.9'14   75-2234
ISBN 0-15-179270-4

First edition

B C D E

POLLY'S

CONTENTS

The Hour of the Tiger

4:00 A.M.

1

In the Rock Hotel in Gibraltar, a man lay on a new white bedspread in a single room overlooking the harbor. The slatted shutters were drawn back, and the November rain slashed at the glass of the window. The man was wide awake, and fully dressed. With his head propped on the pillow he could see out and across the bay towards Algeciras. Each time the storm lit up the disturbed water with a sharp photoflash of blue light, his eyes focused on the outline of a vessel at anchor outside the mole, a submarine.

In the glare of a particularly bright flash the man stirred and swung his legs to the floor. He drew the curtains. The sound of the rain and wind seemed muffled as he walked through to the bathroom. He bathed his hands and face, dried himself, and looked up at his reflection in the glass. To most people it would have seemed the face of a good-looking Japanese in his early thirties, long-necked, with well-kept long hair in the manner of an aging pop singer.

Coming back into the bedroom, the man glanced at his wristwatch. It was just after 4:00 A.M. He walked to the suitcase stand, lifted his case off it onto the bed, and snapped it open. He rummaged for a moment under the neatly piled clothes and drew out a flat black plastic envelope about eighteen inches long and a foot wide. Un-zipping it, he put in his hand and began to take things out and lay them along the coverlet.

First, he took a square of white rough silk and carefully unfolded and spread it out. On top of this he placed a pair of women's panties. Next to the panties he laid a black lacquer scabbard inlaid with silver, from the mouth of which protruded the twined hilt of a short Japanese sword.

An expert would instantly have recognized it as a form of *tanto*, the smallest of the three typical samurai weapons, and the one most frequently used to commit the ritual act of seppuku, more frequently and vulgarly known in the West as hara-kiri.

The man paused for a moment and looked out through the windows at the dark, still lightning-lit expanse of the Spanish sky. Then, as if feeling a need to simplify matters, he zipped up the plastic envelope, replaced it in the suitcase, and lifted the suitcase in his arms and back onto the stand.

Returning to the bed, the man sat down and fingered the lacquer of the scabbard. Then, seeming to make up his mind, he stood up, undressed, and put on the pair of panties, smoothing and stretching them tight over the flesh of his buttocks and belly. Falling to his knees on the carpet, he lifted the sword in both hands. He pressed its coldness across his burning chest, then, with a slow, steady easing movement he began to unsheathe the blade. As it emerged, the light from the bedside lamp gleamed on the surface of the steel and picked out a strange, beautiful wavy line near the edge. It seemed to ripple like the line of clouds along the horizon above the sea.

The man was crying. A salt tear fell on the bright metal

and stood like a jewel, humped, without sliding. The man lifted a corner of the silk square and carefully took it up, as if blotting something very precious. When the tip of the blade left the scabbard, he sighed, letting his breath out. With his right hand he laid the empty scabbard aside on the silk. With his left hand he turned the naked blade and laid it facing away from him on the silk.

The man closed his eyes, kneeling in prayer or meditation before the exposed sword. His lips began to move, but no words came out. As the silent incantation, if such it was, continued, the man began to move the muscles along the upper part of his body. The sinews flexed and tensed, beneath the gleaming sweat on his naked skin, while he seemed gently and rhythmically to be exercising each separate part of himself. The light shone on the ridges of his shoulder blades, on the heart shape of his neck hollow, on the tendons in his forearms and wrists. It was as if a well-made car were being given its annual service, or an autopsy being conducted on a living body.

The man's legs were braced rigid on the floor, tensed and firm, erecting his weaving upper body into its own world of movement. He seemed like two men, an upper man of endless fluidity and change, a lower man of rocklike stability and firmness. There was a kind of schizophrenia of the body, broken into two by the iridescent obscenely bulging woman-silk in the groin. Somehow the pressures seemed to beat against each other, as if the working life and joy of the torso was bearing down on and being beaten back by the iron-hard inanition and massive resistance of the braced legs. Or as if the two were being held apart and thrust upward into a fountaining tower of implacable heaving at the stiff point where the man's pulsing and beating organ was forcing itself against the nylon.

Outside, the storm seemed to ease. The rain was still coming, but the flashes of the lightning seemed for a moment to be getting fainter, as if the storm was receding across the bay. Then, without warning, an intense flash laced the whole sky open. Almost instantly, the thunderclap burst overhead.

The man threw back his head till the tendons in his neck stretched tight. With one smooth lunging movement, he thrust the nylon down from his waist and reared himself above the empty scabbard, stiff-legged, with his huge bucking organ bared like a sword in the fetid air. His eyes locked on the naked, gleaming blade as his hands went about their business, kneading and wrenching powerfully until the thick tortured thing was finally strangled and its white gluey life gulped and oozed out over the silvered lacquer.

Afterwards, he lay back on the coverlet, the sweat slowly drying along his body, the sword still beside him untouched on the white virgin square of silk. It was as if all that mattered about his life, all its gaiety and frivolous vitality, had been used up and expended in one last desperate spree. The day of the scabbard was over.

His body felt cold, as if the planet of his being was edging finally into the darkness. He touched the softness of the light fur on his chest, the more wiry bush around his flaccid parts, the glossiness of the long hair falling over his shoulders.

He knelt again beside the square of silk. He had no eyes

for the mess on the scabbard. His gaze was fixed in a trance-like stare on the light on the blade. It seemed to flicker and beckon, like a presence arrived to direct him to another place, perhaps for judgment, perhaps for reward.

His hand seemed to reach out of its own accord. It took the sword by the rough rattan of the hilt, the sweat-slippery palm held still by the irregular placing of the gilt *menuki* under the twine. His spine seemed to lock into place, upright and firm as a pillar or a gravestone. The muscles of his belly were taut and firm as the point of the blade turned in the air and moved toward the spot a little above the left hip where the man would make the first incision. The coldness of the steel against his flesh made him shiver and frown for a second, but his mind was already in its own dream. Self-hypnotized, he jerked back his head and fixed his eyes on the glare of the bedside lamp, letting his whole spirit sink into the blaze of the filament, as his instructors had told him the celebrant in the rite of seppuku should do. With a steady, unhurried movement, as if resheathing the sword in its scabbard, or entering the body of a young virgin for the first time, he pressed the point home into his body, turned it along its side, and firmly drew it across his stomach to the right hip.

2

It was just after 5:00 A.M. on a cold drizzling morning, and the Soho bookshop was officially closed. The policeman on his beat was an efficient officer, and he had seen the couple arrive, but he had done nothing about it. He knew why they were there. They had arrived separately, the man by chauffeur-driven car, which had dropped him a block away, giving him a short walk through the rain; the girl in an old blue Ferrari she had driven herself.

The man had arrived first, and was leaning reading with his back to the door when he heard the bell, the scrape of the wood, and the click as the door fell back. He didn't turn around. The girl walked lightly up to him and kissed him in the hollow between his left ear and shoulder. As she did so, she allowed her breast to ease forward under his armpit and her belly to press over his buttocks. The man might have smiled, or frowned, or even murmured

Not before briefing, darling, since he had done, as she knew, all three of these things on similar occasions before. Instead, he tapped with his fingers on a much-thumbed copy of *Mayfair* at his elbow.

Must I?

Read it.

The girl pulled him around and kissed him full on the mouth, flexing and rotating her body against his. The man gently pushed her away.

Not before briefing, darling, he said this time. And then, tapping the *Mayfair* again:

Read it.

The girl opened the magazine. Slipped into the center-page spread, and smoothly covering a pair of arched buttocks into which the photographer had ingeniously tucked a crimson tulip, was a carefully typed double-spaced note.

The girl read it through, fast, and without comment or movement.

Very nasty. I didn't think you had it in you.

Never mind about that. I want you to fly to Gibraltar and find out why he did it.

You mean this really happened?

A man stabbed himself two days ago on the Rock in exactly the way he describes.

Who describes?

The man smiled, and inclined his head.

Is this another of Loyola's little games?

He fancies himself as a short-story writer, the man explained.

Jesus Christ.

Let's go and lie down in the back, and we'll work it out.

Valerian, said the girl some time later, you're a bit choppy.

My dear, I've only been up for an hour and a half.

I wish that you had, she said.

They were lying on a low divan that was covered in a sort of white goatskin rug which irritated and at the same time slightly stimulated the skin. They were both naked, and the girl rested with her head in the man's groin. Reflections of what they were doing were endlessly multiplied on all four walls, in the ceiling, and on the floor, since the room was completely surfaced in beige-tinged mirror glass. There was no furniture except for the divan and tubes of dim, opaque-tinted neon lighting which circled the room at the junction of the walls and the floor. Dark shadows flowed and shifted in the hollows and over the mounds of their bodies as the direction and intensity of the light varied. It had taken a computer program of considerable ingenuity to achieve this effect, and Valerian was very proud of it.

I wish you'd keep off my ambiguities, he said.

The girl's head shifted, and her mouth began to move with a soft, octopus sound over the places nearest to it.

I told you, Cadbury, he said.

A little later, when the flickering reflections of her attentions had died away, and the girl had swallowed, the man expelled his breath in a long, contented sigh.

You're good at that, he said.

I'm good at everything, she replied.

Valerian stroked the soft straw of her hair and reflected, not for the first time, on the advantages of the kind of business relationship his job demanded. The girl lay with

her legs apart, in the kind of ungainly, relaxed comfortable-
ness of a young lioness. He watched her stir and stretch in
the ceiling.

Sometimes I think I could almost fall in love with you,
he thought.

But he didn't say this. For Valerian, falling in love was
a fast and cruel business. He remembered the last time still,
and the consequences. It was not for nothing that the Service
had picked him up and taught him detachment.

The girl began to stroke her breasts to and fro across
his belly, advancing her body over his until her parted lips
reached up to his face and her quick tongue stabbed into
his mouth.

You know why we call me Cadbury.

Valerian smiled. He did know. Loyola had wanted something a bit more septic, like Mildred Lush. But the taste for
a name that would whet the appetites had prevailed. The
Service knew which side its bread was buttered on, Valerian
reflected.

Would you like a bite?

The girl had parted her legs and was lying back with
her hands cupped, palms outward, to form an inviting portico
around the lips of her vagina. She was perfect, Valerian
thought. She had an absolutely natural, insatiable sexuality
of a totally undiscriminating kind. As long as a man was
willing, she would do everything she could to excite his
sexual desire. She made no distinction between old and
young, black and white, attractive or apparently ugly. For
Cadbury, no one was ugly. It all became a matter of con-
structing out of the available ingredients the most efficient
piece of machinery for her satisfaction.

I know what you're thinking, she said.
I know that you know what I'm thinking.

They had lain in silence for several minutes. These en-
counters were always, in their own way, a kind of test. She
knew that. Valerian had to reassure himself of her powers.
She had been his choice for the job in the first place, but
he needed the happiness of convincing his doubts.

I also like a good fuck.

I wish you wouldn't read my mind, she said.

The idea for an agent who would use her sex as a man
could use his violence had, of course, been Loyola's. Only
Loyola could have thought up something so macabre.

I want a woman, he had said, leaning back with his feet
on the Wellington chest. I require you, Valerian, to do some
auditions. Though it isn't, of course, exactly a matter of
how they'll *sound*. Or not that only.

Did he really say that?

Cadbury had asked the question more than once when
Valerian had retold the story, as he loved to do. The detail
attracted her. After all, she had said, they might have all
been interviewed in the dark. With just the moans and the
sucking noises to go by.

Well, you weren't.

Indeed, the auditions had taken place in a blaze of
light, as Cadbury remembered. Entering the white oper-
ating theater wearing only a G string and a pair of black
stockings under a starched nurse's apron. Valerian like a
prime bull with nothing on but a dab of Brut.

You knelt at my feet.

I did.

And we managed the whole thing without once falling off the trolley.

Valerian had always had high praise for this.

I still remember that lecherous burst of applause.

You knew you'd get the job.

I did.

Loyola had been delighted. He had taken her out to dinner and fed her shrimps. He had had his hand under her skirt throughout the lemon sherbet. There was no stopping him in the taxi.

Valerian, she's a jewel, he had said the next morning, as he stirred his Alka-Seltzer. It's been almost ten years, as Oscar said. But she managed it.

His spectacles had gleamed with joy.

So Cadbury had become the first sixty-nine agent in the history of the Service. Sixty-nine, of course, had also been Loyola's invention. Sixty-nine, he had said, rubbing his hands. Licensed to screw.

There were times when Valerian regretted this obsession of Loyola's with the more Ian Fleming-ish aspects of their activities. Of course, it had its advantages. In the submission of expense claims, for example.

I think a sort of glass box for the contact point, sir, he had said one day as they sipped their liqueur coffee together in the eighth-floor canteen overlooking Whitehall. I shall need to keep in touch with her. Check on her performance and so on. Mirrors would help.

It had cost a cool three thousand to strip and line the back room, but Loyola had signed the chits without a murmur. The running costs were smaller, of course. The rather blasé succession of out-of-work students and actors who ran the front shop were well-enough paid, but the income from the hard porn below the counter verged on the astronomical. Indeed, there were times when Valerian realized that the Service would eventually make a profit from his luxury. It was a pleasant thought. After all, they were public servants, and they were there to serve. Blunt instruments in the hands of government.

What *is* a public servant, the girl had once asked, as they walked in Trafalgar Square.

A public servant is a servant of the public, Valerian had replied. If they want to fuck you, they fuck you. Or, rather, a selected set of them do, on whom we have certain designs, and from whom we require certain information.

You mean, if they want to fuck the Service, I see they *get* fucked.

It comes to the same in the end, said Valerian, and he had paused by one of the fountains.

I wonder, she said.

All's fair in sex and violence. And we have a job to do.

She remembered how the pigeons had settled on Valerian's head and shoulders as they talked, and the gentleness with which he had stroked their feathers.

The goatskin tickled Valerian. His train of thought was interrupted. He glanced at the Bueche-Giraud on his wrist. It was half past five. With a long swing, he rolled from the bed to the floor, stood up, and stretched. The glass was deliciously cool under his feet. A concealed thermostat allowed him to vary the temperature, and he stood for a moment enjoying the sense of walking like Christ over cold water. He was thinking of how to reintroduce the subject of their meeting to the girl.

A blunt instrument in the hands of government, he said, looking down at his lax penis. More me than you, I should say.

The girl snaked forward, spreading her long fingers under his testicles, but he drew back.

Not now, Cadbury.

I want to be governed, Valerian, she said.

There was no controlling the movements of those long fingers. Valerian was tumescent already.

A sheath, he murmured, for a world of swords.

Then sheathe yourself in me, said Cadbury, and had straddled herself for action. They fucked with a short, convulsive joy, as he stood carrying her in his arms, legs planted wide apart on the mirrors.

Like Atlas lifting the moon, said Cadbury, and they squeezed each other to a shuddering climax.

The point about swords was this, said Valerian later, as they rested with her head on his cheek. Three times, by the way, is too much. I really feel awful.

You had to test me, said Cadbury. Did I pass?

About the swords, he said firmly. A fortnight ago, the most famous Japanese sword in England, perhaps in Western Europe, was stolen from an open showcase at Loyola's old school.

I screwed a boy from there once, said Cadbury. A very proper young man. But he had crabs.

Valerian was used to ignoring Cadbury. It took some time for the ice-cold brain in her warm body to start freezing. But when it did, her concentration was arctic. He continued.

The sword was an early Japanese *katana,* curved and sharpened on one side of the blade. It had a fine, straight tempering line, and a single groove on the ridge.

You sound like a Sotheby's catalogue.

Two days ago, said Valerian, I could have written all I knew about Japanese swords on the back of a silver *habaki.*

Clever, said Cadbury, with a squirm of her belly.

Now, he added, I am by way of being an expert. As you, my delicious Cadbury, he said, disengaging himself, must also be. On the outward side of the tang, or bit that goes inside the hilt, of this sword, there were two incised characters forming the name Yasutsuna. This would, of course, be the name of the smith who forged the blade.

I'm fascinated, said Cadbury. But her body was still, and she sounded really fascinated.

Now there are several smiths who are known to have used this name, often many centuries after the first and most famous one, who worked in the early tenth century.

Before the Battle of Maldon.

Probably. So whatever he made has a certain charm of antiquity. I wish you would let me talk, Cadbury.

She kissed his forehead. Her lips were cool, and he knew she was really starting to listen.

Japanese blades are generally accepted as the top swords in the world. They make the best Toledo stuff seem like amateur work, apparently. And collectors will pay a fortune for the really good examples, like this one at Stowe school.

You said there were several smiths of the same name. How do we know the original one made the sword at Stowe?

Valerian smiled. There was very little that Cadbury missed when she was awake.

I won't bore you with all the details. But the metal was authenticated a few years ago after extensive tests in the Newton Chambers laboratories in Sheffield. They know it's old. Of course, the signature might still be an early forgery, or, more likely, a sort of tribute or act of homage whereby a lesser smith signed the master's name as a way of praising his style. But they've been into that, too. The Japanese Sword Society in Tokyo has examined the chisel marks and compared them favorably with those in the authentic Yasutsuna blades in Japan. So it all looks O.K.

A sort of oriental Excalibur is purloined from a well-known boy's public school, said Cadbury. And a man disembowels himself in Gibraltar. It's Fu Manchu stuff. How was it done?

I'm coming to that, said Valerian. But first let me give you an idea of why. The value of these things is really quite extraordinary. Some years ago, John Yumoto devised a sort of collector's comparative price guide, whereby he gave a value of five to a basic *katana* blade in good condition by one of the least-famous smiths. Taking this as a base, he evaluated blades by a thousand other smiths at figures ranging up to six hundred. Now on this scale, a blade by the first Yasutsuna is listed at two seventy. That means that you could expect to pay at auction about fifty-four times as much for a good blade by Yasutsuna as for one by Joe Bloggs.

I love your Anglo-Saxon analogies, said Cadbury.

All right, said Valerian, absently brushing her nipple with his palm, and scarcely noticing when she stopped him. At

Christie's last November, a number of swords by Joe Bloggs were going for five or six hundred pounds. Work it out for yourself.

At a conservative estimate, said Cadbury, the Yasutsuna sword from Stowe would have been expected to fetch about twenty-five thousand pounds.

Right, said Valerian. You'd think they could well have afforded to drop the school fees. But they didn't. And they don't really seem to have quite realized what an expensive little toy they had on their hands. They had it up for grabs in a simple locked glass showcase in the Assembly Hall, and apparently nobody bothered tuppence about it. Until one day the Headmaster had a letter from a well-known Japanese collector about to visit England on holiday, asking if he might come along and examine the sword. English politeness prevailed, and an invitation was issued.

I know what happened next, said Cadbury, with her cheeks cupped in her hands. She lay belly downwards on the floor, rotating herself against her own reflection.

Why have you gone so far aw y, said Valerian, who had failed to notice when she rolled from his side on the bed.

He arrived with a Thompson submachine gun, said Cadbury, with her eyes half closed. My pubic hair is itchy. Massacred the whole of the sixth form at morning prayers, buggered the head prefect, and swept off with the sword in a 1928 Bentley.

He found the sword had already gone.

Cadbury rolled onto her back and began to pedal her legs in the air.

You mean the case was empty, and nobody had noticed? No.

Another sword had been substituted, and nobody had noticed?

Exactly.

Give her the money, said Cadbury, and began to scissor her legs out and in, as if being forcefully assaulted by an invisible gorilla.

When you've quite finished, said Valerian, shall we take a break and have some coffee?

The amazing thing is, said Valerian, that he saw the sword was the wrong one from twenty yards away.

They were sitting opposite each other at a small, Formica-topped table in a café in Covent Garden. Porters and fruit-sellers were discussing prices and shortages.

It wasn't the right length, he went on. The one they'd substituted was a foot shorter. The trouble is that to Western eyes all Japanese swords, like Japanese women, tend to look exactly alike. They have the same curve and the same edge.

I doubt that women's lib would thank you for that.

It's true. They're all gray in the dark, as they say. You can't pick them out. But the natives can.

And this "well-known Japanese collector," said Cadbury, shaking her hair away from her saucer, was able to spot the theft at once.

He was.

And so, said Cadbury, Loyola would like me to go to Gibraltar and find out why this beautiful Japanese who attempts suicide was involved with the pretty sword that got stolen from the old school. Sounds like a misappropriation of public funds.

Just so, said Valerian. But you know Loyola.

I do, said Cadbury. I do indeed.

They finished their awful coffee in silence. Outside, a church clock chimed six. It was the hour of the hare.

The Hour of the Hare
6:00 A.M.

3

When the telephone rang, Cadbury was still asleep. It sounded angrier and angrier as her arm poured out of the bedclothes to lift it from its cradle.

Your alarm call, it said.

She glanced at her wristwatch on its white leather band, all she was wearing. It was six o'clock.

The hour of the hare, she thought, clasping her hands behind her neck and staring at the ceiling.

Alexis, she called. Where are you, boy?

She felt a coldness against her neck, and the rough feel of fur brushing her face.

Alexis. They wanted to kill you, baby.

She slid her fingers along the crushed bone of the borzoi's rib cage, enjoying, as she always did in the morning, his incredible slimness and tension. He was like a piece of furniture, she had once thought, something constructed out of ivory for an Indian potentate, and hung with expensive tapestry. Except that he moved. Like a deer. Or like a Ferrari.

In my dream you were being attacked by a Japanese with a sword. He looked like Loyola, or like my father. I was very frightened.

The dog looked into her face with his beautiful, noble

eyes. His head lightly pushed her breast, so that she lost her balance and fell away from him on the pillows. He reached down and licked her eyes.

Yes, but you foxed him. Yes, you did.

Her lips formed a kiss for him.

You turned into a beautiful woman.

The dog collapsed himself into an elegant curve beside her on the floor, with his tongue slightly protruding and his eyes looking up devotedly.

And when he wanted to fuck you, the bell rang. And I woke up. And you were here.

She leaned down, letting her long hair fall onto his head as her hands played with his neck and ears.

Alexis, she said. We must have our bath. The airplane takes off at nine, and I have to pack. I shall be in Gibraltar by lunchtime.

The dog listened attentively. Alexis had always possessed this attractive power to seem more relaxed and at ease when you told him what you were thinking. So Cadbury had come to discuss her most intimate problems with him. He was like a psychiatrist, she reflected.

In what way, her psychiatrist had once asked.

He certainly hasn't your physique, Magneto.

Magneto had smiled. His air of a sort of Polynesian chieftain was carefully cultivated. He swapped it sometimes for a look of Picasso snapped on the beach at Nice in his early eighties. This one demanding shirts open to the waist and a revelation of black chest hair and trinkets. Cadbury adored him.

You had better beware of your dog, he had said. He may learn to talk.

Well, so may you, Magneto. And then, where *would* the Service be?

Alexis was hungry. She always knew that his appetites were stirring when he rose, as he now did, and arched his back like a cat stretching sleep out of itself.

We have to wash first, she said.

The dog loped ahead of her through the sliding doors at the end of the room. He paused, watching her follow him in across the Italian tiles.

The bathroom had been installed for Cadbury on the same expense scale as Valerian's contact point. As the tinted water flooded from ivory taps into its kidney-shaped recessed basin in the floor, she remembered the mild hassles there had been over some of her more eccentric details.

I can see the case for one bidet, said Loyola. But *two*.

Supposing we have a woman guest. And we're in a hurry, darling. And besides, it looks more symmetrical.

She had had her way. Not least because Valerian had seen the advantages of a threesome while Cadbury was on duty abroad, and had put in a strong word on her behalf. As the cool fountain freshened and fell back on the porcelain, she reflected on the joys of female companionship.

It's so nice watching someone else, Alexis, she said. I do so wish that you were a bitch sometimes.

The borzoi watched the pool begin to fill and bubble. He dipped his paw in as his mistress dried between her legs. Apart from the two bidets, there was nothing else in the room except the recess of the bath in the floor, and a long shelf behind it covered with baskets of soap, sponges, and loufas. On either side of the door, however, in the wall facing this shelf, there were two small circular apertures, slightly hooded and able to rotate through a very wide angle. Fitted into the plaster behind these were a powerful movie camera and a projector. When Cadbury stepped down into the water and reached up to turn off the taps, a film of herself on the bidet began to unroll across the ceiling. With a sort of narcissistic pleasure, she floated and watched her accomplished manipulation of her body.

Why does a man masturbate before he kills himself, said Cadbury, as she started to wash. I'll tell you, Alexis. He does it to empty himself, and also to sum up his life. I knew a boy once who said you could measure out your life in orgasms. They gave you so many, and when they were all used up, you were finished. The problem was, to find out the total amount of your ration. A man in Gibraltar a week ago had reached the end, so he thought he would have his last climax. And then he put the point of a blade in his belly, and let his guts out. I wonder why.

Alexis laid his head on his paws, as if he was thinking.

That, said Cadbury, is what we are going to find out in Gibraltar. I wish you could come, she added, fondling the dog's ears with a soapy hand.

The film of her bath unrolled with a quiet flickering sound on the ceiling. She lay in the warm scented water, relaxed and soporific. She saw her hands moving with sinewy precision over the glistening inlets and porticoes of her body, the intimate renewal of her own caresses of herself. The dog panted at her shoulder. He, too, was watching.

Alexis, she said quietly. I think you need a wash.

At the word "wash," the dog shivered slightly, as if some

special nerve center in his brain had been alerted for action. He stretched a little.

Cadbury reared herself from the water and put her nose into the borzoi's long fur along his belly. Mmm, yes. You do need a wash, she said.

She took a fresh bar of Chanel from a basket and dipped it into the water. With a slow, easy movement she began to rub the bar up and down along the dog's belly. He started to growl, a low, deep sound far back in his throat.

There, boy. There, there. It's only a wash.

At the second mention of the word "wash," this time pronounced with a soft, dwelling sound on the final consonants, the dog stirred and shivered. The girl increased the speed and roughness of her movements, dipping the wet bar again into the water.

Only a wash. Only a wash, she said softly.

The dog began to shudder, growling continuously now as her hands moved more freely in strong, firm movements over his whole body, soaping and manipulating his fur.

With a deft skillfulness, she slipped her fingers between the dog's back legs, reaching for his penis. Gently, she began to knead and caress it, soaping the head and the cavities below the foreskin. Her hands moved with a slow delicate skill, then quicker, and quicker still, as the dog's organ began to harden and erect.

Needs washing, washing. It needs washing, she began to intone in a steady rhythmical whisper.

The dog reared. With a sudden violent jerk, it pulled itself away from those passionate fingers. But the girl was ready. In a single, quick sinewy movement she had slithered her body under his, opened her thighs, and swung up her pelvis towards him. Her arms and hands pressed back on the slippery tiles, and she locked her legs at the ankles firmly round the dog's back, thrusting her vulva against the firm head of his sex.

I want you to wash me, wash me, boy, she moaned.

At each repetition of the word wash, she forced her body energetically up against the dog's as his hard slender pink organ entered her vagina. It took about seventeen strokes, her breath coming in short heavy gasps, while she struggled to support her weight and keep the dog inside her. At the last, feeling Alexis start to shudder into his climax, she clutched herself convulsively to him and dragged them by sheer strength over and into the water. She came to her orgasm as they sank together into splashing darkness.

Alexis, she said later, while the film of their washing unrolled on the ceiling, I think I love you. More than Valerian.

The dog lay on the tiles in the corner, steaming a little in the heat, with his long head on his paws.

Love is a luxury. Like snails and oysters, she continued. And today I only have time for brewer's yeast.

The episode with the dog, she reflected, as she rose from the bath and began to dry herself, was good practice. In her business, it was necessary to contain a piece of sexual machinery in her body as effective and well oiled as a high-powered rifle. She had always to be quick on the draw. Able to moisten her lips at a moment's notice, and for man, woman, or beast.

It's a dog's life, Alexis, she said, as she toweled vigorously. A bitch's life. A man can pull his gun and shoot to kill. I just have to spread my legs and take it. Even from you, she added, reaching down to kiss the dog lightly on the forehead.

Even from you, she said again later, watching the dog in the kitchen. He was completely absorbed in the business of eating, as oblivious to the implications of their earlier encounter in the bathroom as if it had never happened.

Just like a man, she said affectionately.

For Alexis the world had become a place of raw steak, a vendetta between his teeth and a dead, savory animal, in which this woman had no part. He ate like a cat, voraciously, with a sort of cruel, dedicated persistence. Afterwards, he coughed, and sighed. Then he loped through to the bedroom and flung himself on a rug in front of the fire.

Cadbury followed him through, with the glass of brewer's yeast mixed with water in her hand, but the dog was already half asleep. He was like a cat in the way a Siamese was like a dog, a half-creature of mingled affection and waywardness, she thought. Cadbury loved him.

I have to go soon, Alexis, she said. Madame will see you're fed.

The telephone rang again while she was packing. She turned from the pile of underclothes and open cases with a sigh.

Yes, she said.

There's just one thing I forgot to tell you, said Valerian. The man who slit his stomach on the Rock didn't succeed in killing himself. He's alive and rather unwell in the General Hospital. So you might like to drop in and take him some paper flowers.

Valerian.

Yes, Cadbury.

This is an obscene telephone call. I'd like to unzip your jeans, pull your prick out, and chop it off with a *wakizashi*.

You've been doing some reading.

Why couldn't you tell me the whole story before?

Valerian began to breathe heavily.

I'd like to take down your pretty little peach knickers, he began.

But Cadbury had hung up. It took her another thirty minutes to finish her packing, put on a face, and ask the French prostitute who ran the brothel downstairs to look after Alexis. The dog was still asleep as she closed the door and went out into the London sun.

4

In the taxi out to the airport Cadbury sat back and began to enjoy herself. It was always the same. She had this indefinable sense of being on a holiday whenever she set off on a job abroad. However grim or boring the immediate future might look, she could never overcome her initial feeling of freedom. Even the beat-up studio houses along the road towards Hammersmith were less drab and uninviting than usual.

The taxi accelerated from an amber light, and they began to climb the overpass. In the other direction the rush-hour traffic had yet to build up, and there was still a sense of purpose and movement in the flow of cars into London. It was a bright, crisp morning, and the sun gave their chrome-and-metal surfaces an extra glitter. Cadbury fingered the zippers of her calf suitcases on the seat beside her. It was even a nice-enough day to be staying. Visit Fortnum and Mason's for a slice of orange cake or a frappé. Spend the afternoon with Ian at Vanilla, and have her hair washed. Perhaps even a walk in Hyde Park to feed the ducks. She could lie on the grass under the trees in the sun, and look up at the sky with her eyes closed. Except that someone would try to pick her up.

It was curious, Cadbury reflected, how sex always reared its ugly head. She appreciated this metaphor. It seemed to convey the quality of male aggressiveness and unthinking pride. It was amazing how men exaggerated the importance of the thing itself. Or, rather, the sheer size of it. Never its proportions, or whether it worked properly. The one thing that seemed to interest their fantasies was whether it was big enough for the places it had to go in.

She felt a twinge of remembered irritation between her legs, and eased her thighs on the seat. It happened so often. One had to be a self-lubricating mechanism. Ahead of her, to the left, as she shifted her position, she could see the tall dull glass slab of the Gillette building in Brentford. She drew the taxi window down a little, and shook her hair in the stab of cold air that rushed in.

I wonder if the Japanese are good at making razor blades, she thought. Or whether they rely on inspiration from ours.

Her train of thought was rudely interrupted when the taxi braked suddenly, flinging her forward sharply. There was a fierce blast on the horn as the car again accelerated. Ahead of them the low-profile back of a sports car was disappearing at speed, with a high roar from its exhaust.

Bleeding Datsun, said the taxi driver through the glass panel. Stupid fucker. Think they know it all. Think they know it all.

What happened, said Cadbury.

Datsun fucking sports, said the driver. Just cut across without a signal. Cut across.

The Japanese car was again changing lanes, snaking over to the slow lane and then back to avoid an obstinate truck.

See what I mean, said the driver. Think they fucking know it all. He'll kill himself, and serve him fucking right.

Was he Japanese?

The Datsun was out of sight, lost far ahead in the stream of traffic unreeling onto the M4.

Kamikaze, said Cadbury.

And camiknickers to you, too, love, said the driver. His good humor was evidently restored by this *trouvaille*. Cadbury firmly slid the glass panel back. She knew too well what this kind of conversation always led to, and she wanted to think.

At Heathrow she checked her bags in, bought some magazines, and walked down the long ramp to the departure gate. As she waited in the queue for a boarding ticket, she glanced around at her fellow-passengers. Most of those traveling on BE 4309 to Gibraltar were middle-aged couples on a tour. They were loaded with cameras and binoculars, incongruously dressed in open-necked shirts and bright pant-suits. There were several students, all hair and anoraks, and a handful of neat men with briefcases. Almost all the men eyed Cadbury with either disguised or frankly covetous lustfulness. The women stared at her clothes as if they hoped embarrassing stains would suddenly appear all over them.

Cadbury expected this. She knew she was worth looking at. She was wearing a chamois leather skirt from Skin, in the King's Road, and a matching chamois shirt, with sleeves close-fitting on the upper arms and flaring at the wrists. The neckline was cut very low and laced across with chamois strips. Her boots were skin-tight matching suède, zippered to the knee. Underneath these she wore nothing except a pair of black silk panties specially cut to fit her. Most of the men had arrived at this conclusion on the basis of exterior evidence alone.

It was always her practice to sort out the possibles before she boarded. You could always manage to sit where you were easy of access.

I have a bit of a headache. Could you give me a window seat by myself, she said to the steward. She smiled, and let her hair fall over his hand.

Of course, he said, solicitous and lustful.

Thank you so much.

She bent to pick up her traveling bag, leaning outward

slightly towards a particular man she had noticed ignoring her. This was always intriguing, and besides, there was something else about him. He was Japanese.

George, said a middle-aged woman.

I'm sorry, dear.

We're not here to study leather goods.

The Japanese was across the aisle, in the row behind. He was good-looking in a strange, exotic way, well dressed in a cheap stylish cotton suit and an open-necked shirt. He looked tough, and rich.

Might as well keep in practice, Cadbury thought.

She settled herself on the cushion, fiddled with her seat belt, shook out her hair, and began to read.

Although she had bought a spray of magazines—*Harper's, Guns and Ammo,* and *Penthouse*—she had no intention of doing more than use them as bait. It attracted men to see a woman with a magazine published for their own sex. *Guns and Ammo* was always a winner on transatlantic flights. *Penthouse* she regarded as a faithful stand-by. *Harper's* was useful for the shy type. She had already classified the Japanese as a *Guns and Ammo* case.

She began to flick over the pages, inspecting the ads for facsimiles with a bored eye. She stopped at an article on the new 9mm Smith and Wesson 14-shot automatic. The gun lay on a bed of golden cartridges, its black muzzle thrusting invitingly forward from the page. Cadbury tilted the magazine to allow this alluring symbolism to catch the eye of anyone looking over her shoulder.

She was fairly sure that the man in the seat behind must

have noticed her. The only question was when he would make his move.

I'll bet he was the bastard in the Datsun, she thought.

When breakfast was served, the Trident was flying at thirty thousand feet above an even bed of strato-cumulus. As Cadbury glanced through the flat oval of the window, she caught occasional glimpses of broken fields and the dots of houses in the gaps between the solid-looking fluff. They were over northern Spain, heading at five hundred miles per hour for the last British outpost at the gates of the Atlantic.

Cadbury ate her rolls and processed cheese with relish. Even the coffee seemed tolerable. It was the kind of high that flying always gave her. Everything seemed a little detached from normal reality, and more attractive and beautiful than usual. She reached up and twisted the plastic nipple in the ceiling rack to allow a thin jet of fresh air to gush down on her forehead.

That's the second time today, she thought. I'm becoming an air addict. I must tell Magneto.

But she knew that Magneto would be more interested in what was about to happen between her and the man in the seat behind. She felt a slight sweating between her thighs, as if he were a fighter pilot closing in for the kill, ready to rake her body with a seven-second lethal burst.

I like the image, Magneto would say. And what happened then?

Cadbury finished her coffee and wiped her face with the tiny wet towel so usefully supplied with the sugar and powdered cream. It cooled her brow. She reflected that the time had come for further temptation. Folding *Guns and Ammo* open at a picture of a girl firing a Colt .22 with a shoulder-height two-handed grip assisted by a man in sunglasses, she edged into the aisle and turned to walk back towards the toilet. That should do it, she thought.

The Japanese was looking out the window. He paid no attention as Cadbury swayed past.

Fuck you, mate, she said to herself. The rest of the passengers appraised her with despair and joy. She reached the toilet, eased the folding door open, and slipped in out of sight.

Inside the tiny cabinet, she mouthed at herself for a moment in the mirror above the basin.

I'll have you yet, she said. I'll have you yet, you arrogant bastard.

She lifted her skirt, slid her panties down to her knees, and pissed fiercely into the bowl. A hot orange stream lashed the aluminum. As she finished, she lifted her right leg, tucked the toe in the crutch-piece of the silk, and twitched the expensive material down to her ankles.

Stooping, she picked the panties up and pushed them out of sight in her handbag. She allowed her skirt to skate down over her hips and smoothed it close with her hands. She felt stripped for action.

The seat fell to, and the toilet flushed with a subdued hissing sound.

On the way back to her seat, Cadbury began to count the paces. At the sixth, she put her left foot in front of her right ankle and tripped herself neatly forward across the arm of the empty seat beside her own. Her head and body fell forward, her belly supported itself comfortably on the armrest, and her buttocks (she fully believed) were for a brief second entirely laid bare to the man she was trying to attract.

She was quick to smooth her skirt back, recover her balance, and slide easily into her seat. It had all happened very fast. But the man must have seen.

If he can resist that, he's a homosexual, she reflected as she lay back and closed her eyes. He's certainly good-looking enough.

Beside her, on the spare seat, her traveling case and the open copy of *Guns and Ammo* lay apparently where she had left them.

As the Trident started to lose altitude, Cadbury began to believe that nothing, after all, was going to happen. Or not, at any rate, before they landed. She had slept for a few minutes and waked with a slight pain in her ears to find that the flight was nearly over. She had swallowed and felt her head clear when the huge plane began to drop slowly down through the clouds.

They were coming in over mountains now, the nose dropping and turning a little so that the landscape twisted and slithered away into a corner of her field of vision. There was a sudden burst of the engines, and the wings leveled again. They seemed to be heading again towards open sea. Then again the Trident banked, and Cadbury saw the long ridge of the promontory a mile or two away to their right. They were flying alongside the Rock on the Mediterranean side.

She watched the sheer face of the cliff, and a curious gray even slide in the middle, whose purpose she could not, for the moment, identify.

As the Trident banked again to pass around the point, Cadbury leaned over to look down into the vivid blue of the sea. She felt the tight skin of the chamois stretch on her buttocks. She began to imagine another pressure, the rough feel of cloth on the backs of her bare legs, and an arm stretching around her waist and down to finger up her skirt. She licked her lips, imagining something rubbing on her pubic hair, and then pressing down to her groin.

Her fantasy began to take over. She relaxed against the Japanese's body as he knelt behind her, apparently looking out, as she was, at the view of Gibraltar spread out through the right-hand porthole on the sea below. While the houses and ships flowed past through the glass, glistening and bright in the sharp Mediterranean sun, she pictured the man's powerful fingers working their way steadily into her body. She forced herself to continue looking down at the bay, at the tugs and the three cruisers, at the gray bulk of the submarine, on the decks of which a group of ratings was at work. She tried to keep quiet, pressing her lips in a firm line, squirming only with the middle of her body.

When the Trident dipped again, and the long landing strip came into view between the Rock and La Linea, she imagined the man quickening his strokes like a rower in sight of the shore. She could scarcely contain her need to cry out, to turn and thrust her whole body onto something hard. As the wheels of the plane came down and began to kiss and brush the ground, she began to feel the convulsions of her climax. But she was interrupted with a jerk, frustrated and unsatisfied, when the Trident rolled to a halt in front of the airport lounge.

Dreaming is also practice, she reflected as she watched the other passengers filing down the aisle towards the door.

The Japanese was some distance ahead, walking with his two cases and a golf bag over his shoulder. At the door, he looked around, and his eyes caught and held Cadbury's for a moment. He inclined his head, and smiled.

You bastard, she thought. You must have seen my buttocks writhing and done fuck all about it.

She edged herself into the aisle.

Dear Loyola, she said to herself. The things we do for your old school.

And she stepped lightly down the ramp onto the only remaining strip of British soil on the mainland of Europe.

THE HOUR OF THE DRAGON
8:00 A.M.

5

The man who had tried to kill himself lay unconscious under a plastic tent with a zipper in its side in a private room at the General Hospital near Rosia Bay. Above his head from its stand the shaken blood from a glass bottle dripped into his arm through a rubber tube. Outside the window to his left the morning sun shone on the red, white, and blue houses and the fishing boats in the harbor from which Nelson had sailed to Trafalgar.

In the corridor outside the room, the policeman on duty eased his heavy weight on the hard wooden chair they had given him. He fingered the Colt rim-fire revolver in his leather holster with an unaccustomed sense of incongruity. He wasn't used to fire arms. In particular, he wasn't used to guarding men who were dying anyway. And foreigners at that. The nurses were fun, and the job was a sinecure, but he hadn't joined the force to sit indoors all day.

The man he was guarding lay with a slit four inches wide across his stomach. Several doctors had agreed that the depth of the incision must have demanded exceptional strength and courage for a self-inflicted wound. They had even rung up the Central Casualty Hospital in Osaka, where the experts had been surprised. The Japanese were unusually good at this sort of thing, but this man was evidently a master.

He lay now bandaged from the chest to the groin, his eyes closed and his regular features composed into a ritual mask. A watch ticked at his ear on a gold strap, laid aside on the bedside table. Its hands registered the time as eight o'clock. It was three days and three and a half hours since the man had made the incision in his belly. On the third day, it had reached the hour of the dragon, and he was still alive.

It was Valerian who had insisted on the armed guard. It had cost Loyola a good deal of face with Branch 9, who preferred to be left to run the Empire (or what was left of it, as Valerian cynically remarked) on their own. But the guard had been agreed to. To Valerian it had seemed more than probable that a man who cut his own belly open with a blade as sharp as a razor would expect to achieve the results he aimed at. When he recovered consciousness, if he did, he was highly likely to seize the first available weapon to finish himself off with.

I doubt it, Emerson had said. They tend to feel rather differently about it when they wake up, you know.

This man is a Japanese, said Valerian.

He knew that Emerson fancied himself as an amateur analyst, and the argument could go on for hours.

The suicide statistics, said Emerson, adjusting his horn-rimmed spectacles.

Are bollocks, said Loyola, who could often be rather surprisingly Anglo-Saxon. I agree with Valerian. These chaps just aren't like us. When Tojo missed the mark with his blunderbuss in '45, he was pretty shaken up, they tell me.

Had a circle drawn in lipstick round his nipple, but the bullet failed to nick his heart. He was full of shame.

Times change, said Emerson, but he agreed to the guard.

This guard watched now as the nurse approached him down the corridor. She was carrying a tray with a cup of coffee on it, and her hips swayed gently. She was moving slowly to avoid spilling any. The guard was ready for his coffee. He had asked for some ten minutes ago, and he eyed the steaming Styrofoam with almost as much affection as he did the nurse herself.

Good girl, he said, as he took the cup, and appraised her figure. Frets the brain, this kind of duty.

The girl smiled and leaned the tray on the wall.

He may not last long, she said.

Wonder why he did it. When the world's so full of pretty girls like you, he added, fingering the walnut stock of the Colt.

I wonder, she said. Now I have to take his temperature. So get on with your coffee, and keep your thoughts to yourself.

The policeman grinned as she pushed open the door, shaking her thermometer.

Inside the room, the man still lay on his back, breathing steadily, with the blood dripping from the tube into his arm. The girl paused for a moment in the doorway, running her eye over the bare furnishings of the room. A bedside table. Screens against the wall. A cupboard for clothes and medicine by the window. Nothing very much for a suicide attempt.

She crossed to the window and looked out. The room was

on the first floor, again at Valerian's request. It didn't take much imagination to realize that a quick fall from several stories above ground level might be the best way of completing the suicide.

As the girl turned from the window, she wondered if what she was going to do was justified. She shook the thermometer and approached the bed. The man was breathing steadily. She ran her left hand over the clean contours of his face. The skin felt hot and a little dry. It was a good-looking face, and she enjoyed a guilty sense of voyeurism when she stared frankly down at it.

Tucking the thermometer into the man's mouth, she stood back. Then she bent over him and unloosened the sheets from the other side of the bed, pulling them back to lay bare his bandaged upper body. His chest gently heaved as he continued to breathe in his coma.

Even through the bandages the girl could see the tense muscularity of the man's arms and pectorals. She reached down and drew the pajama bottoms away from his belly and groin, tugging them under his dead weight to ruck them over his knees. The man lay without moving, totally exposed to whatever she was going to do.

The girl panted a little with the effort of moving the man's body. She swallowed. He was going to die, anyway. She reached out her hand and began to caress the dry, hairy pouch of his testicles. She concentrated.

It isn't really a corpse, she said. It's a man. Just like any other man. Except that he tried to kill himself. And he's going to die. He wanted to kill himself, and he's going to die.

A rhythm began to form itself in her mind. She let her

fingers move with it, scampering over the man's genitals to the rough bandage over his belly.

He has to die, she thought. He has to die.

Outside the window, the sun poured like honey on the fertile plants and flowers over the hillside behind the bay. The little boats rocked on the water, and the sound of boys laughing and talking carried into the room. The girl reached out and touched the man with her other hand. Her ten fingers moved like a surgeon's into the vents and interstices of his sex.

He has to live, she thought. He has to live.

The words of a prayer remembered from her childhood in the little church at Otterburn when her father had died came back to her.

I can make you live again by the power of love, she murmured, pressing her lips to the ear of the man on the bed. Her cool hand encircled the shaft of his limp penis. Rhythmically, she began to pull and ease back, shifting the foreskin over the lax muscle with a steady movement.

You have to live, she said. You have to live.

The words moved hypnotically in the stilled air of the room. The clothes of the girl rustled as her hands went to and fro. Her mind focused like a microscope into the body far away in the coffin in Northumberland.

Live, Father. Live, she said.

There was a sudden tension in the man's shoulders. A slight noise seemed to come from his throat. The girl smiled, and licked her tongue swiftly along the lobe of his ear.

Alive, man, alive, she said.

Ten minutes later, as she washed her hands in the doctor's

office, the reaction set in. A sudden fit of nausea caught her, and she felt her mouth fill with vomit.

Have a seat, the little Genoese said. You'd better rest a moment.

Cadbury spat in the sink, and turned to face him, wiping her mouth on a tissue.

I told you it would work, she said. I know what sex can do to men.

The idea had come to her the previous evening, when she had stood at the end of the bed and looked down for the first time at the strange living corpse of the Japanese who had brought her to Gibraltar. The room had been dark except for the thin beam of a bedside lamp on his face. He had seemed already to be part of the darkness, exactly as her father had.

I could masturbate him back to life, she had said.

The doctor had taken an hour to persuade, and a bottle of bad Spanish burgundy. But he had had to agree to the attempt.

And did he say what you want, he now asked.

Cadbury swung her black-stockinged legs from the edge of his desk.

I'd like to change, she said. I have to see the Inspector in an hour. You've really been very helpful.

The doctor smiled resignedly. He was used to the reticence of the military. On the Rock you learned to keep your mouth shut, even when more or less told to do so by a girl young enough to be your daughter.

What happened was this, said Cadbury.

She was sitting with Ritornello Piangi, Chief Superintendent of Police in the British colony of Gibraltar. Ritornello came from a family of Genoese who had emigrated to the Rock shortly after the British occupation in 1709, and he regarded himself as a pillar of the local nobility. He was a small, quick, dark man, with a special Italian severity.

The idea of the Service investigating the suicide with a woman had struck him as typical of the British, but the idea of them investigating it with a woman as young and good-looking as Cadbury had struck him as wayward. The skill with which she had outshot him at clay-pigeon shooting the previous afternoon and the brutality with which she had turned down his offer of bed the previous evening had caused him to revise his opinion.

I'd fuck you anytime, she had said. But not on business. Not because I don't mix pleasure with business. I do. Pleasure very often is business in this job, anyway. But it isn't for you. And I don't believe you could have it off with me and still take me seriously. So you'll have to wait. And I mean wait. So just take your mind completely off it until we've finished work. Or else you won't get my knickers down at all. And I know you'd like to. And you know I'd like you to. So wait. O.K.?

This kind of speech had demoralized more men than Cadbury liked to remember. But it usually worked. And it did here. She could talk to Piangi as detachedly as she could to her grandmother. They were in his office now, a converted hotel bedroom crowded with files and trays in a rickety eighteenth-century terrace house overlooking Algeciras Bay.

I gave him the treatment, said Cadbury. For some time, he seemed to be stiffened up in a kind of heavy sleep. His shoulders and cheek muscles twitched but the rest of his body remained pretty much as it was. Lax and dead. Except, of course, for his prick. Then, when he had his climax, his eyes opened for a moment in a kind of fit and he went very red and tense, and he said something. One word. Twice.

She looked up at Piangi thoughtfully.

The word was "Ieyasu." Now Ieyasu Tokugawa was a famous Japanese shogun in the early seventeenth century.

And what's a shogun, said Piangi.

Boss. Emperor substitute. King of the castle. In his case the first to establish a completely new era of peace and isolation, which lasted for about 250 years. Until the Americans arrived in 1853.

So why did he say Ieyasu?

I wonder, said Cadbury.

When the telephone rang a few minutes later, Piangi had just finished giving Cadbury a further rerun of the exact circumstances in which the dying man had been discovered. How the chambermaid had received no answer to her knocking. How she had used her key to enter the room. How she had come upon the naked bleeding man in the iridescent panties, the sperm-soaked scabbard, and the blood-soaked sword lying beside him on the bed.

Excuse me, he said.

The telephone spoke at some length to Piangi.

All right, he said. We'll be over there.

He was already halfway through the door when Cadbury began to ask him what was the matter.

A few minutes ago, said Piangi, the Japanese was found

dead. There was a lot of blood about. He seems to have been beheaded.

They drove without speaking, the old Ford screeching around the bends and over the humps on the road to Rosia.

It's obvious what must have happened, said the little Genoese as he led them into his office. It's obvious, but it doesn't make sense. He was killed by a single stroke from some kind of heavy cutting weapon. The head was completely severed at the junction of the neck and the scapula.

It must have made a nasty mess of the bedclothes, said Cadbury.

It would have. Yes. Imagine trying to hack someone's head off with a sort of guillotine as he lay face up on a pillow. You'd go right through the bed.

They're made of iron, said Piangi. But, yes. There would have to be blood on the sheets.

And the head would lie where it was. And the body stay on the bed. So he must have been killed on the floor.

Unless he was moved, said Cadbury. She had gone to the window and was watching an orderly push a trolley across a small courtyard.

There would still be blood on the sheets, said the doctor. Quite a lot of blood, I should say. And blood on the man who killed him, too.

Or woman.

Cadbury was always inclined to be feminist when the possibilities of violence were under discussion.

I doubt very much if a woman could have done this job with a single blow. Or many men, for that matter, either.

So let's assume, said Cadbury, that we're dealing with someone pretty out of the ordinary, and include the possibility of a sort of female amazon, or gorilla.

I wish you wouldn't be quite so a priori, said Piangi.

A nurse came in with a plastic tray and three cups of coffee. She put it down on the doctor's desk, looked at Cadbury, and went out. Cadbury was beginning to feel randy. The sight of the young Spanish girl's hips under her starched apron had started a familiar train of thought in her body. She remembered the first occasion when she had been seduced by a woman. The rough cape thrown so casually over her knees in the empty Métro carriage at Clignancourt. The bony, soap-smelling hand running over her lip. And then its shocking, revelatory gallop along the silk of her teen-age stockings and over the garter clasp to the bare hot flesh of her thighs.

Are you still with us, Cadbury, said Piangi.

Violence always makes me excited, said Cadbury as she

lowered herself to the one armchair in the office and reached for coffee. I was just remembering how I first got turned on by an old nurse in Paris.

Do you fancy Carminetta, said the little Genoese.

She's too young, said Cadbury, stirring her coffee. For me it has to be older if it's a woman.

They were all disturbed by the sudden murder of the Japanese, and all had tried to disguise it. For the doctor, a whole stream of technicalities had been needed to mask the sheer outrage of a death by violence in a hospital. He was used to death, but he existed to try to prevent it. A man who had nearly ended his own life by a brutal self-incision had been skillfully nursed back to the way to recovery. And an unknown professional destroyer had broken into his own world of caring and reduced his work to nothing. He felt insulted, and very angry. But what he showed was a sort of methodical detachment.

For Cadbury, as she watched him drink his coffee, the symptoms were familiar. She felt a flush of pity for him, and a sense of annoyance with herself for being so superficial and jokey.

It really is a bloody business, she said. You must forgive me, Doctor, for being so logical. It's self-protective. I get a sort of ghoulish high when I think of limbs and things chopped off, and there's no point in denying it. It makes me want some perverse sex. Perhaps to make up for it.

You gave him his last orgasm, said Piangi.

The death of the Japanese had excited his hunting instinct. He wanted another death, the blood of the man who had done it. He felt aggressive, and anxious to press the world in its weakest places. This pretty little English bitch included.

I know, said Cadbury as she swallowed the last of her coffee. It was history repeating itself.

You mean that he jerked off before? When he put the knife in his own belly.

I do.

So he knew, said Piangi, sarcastically, as he struck a match and lit a Caporal, that a man with a chopper was going to drop from the clouds and finish him off ten minutes after the nurse had been with his bedpan.

Be serious, said Cadbury. I've been realizing that my theory didn't work. He didn't come to life because of the skill I used in stroking him. Though I wanted to think he would. He let me draw him off because he knew what was coming. And he wanted to make himself ready for it as he'd done before. He needed the purification of sexual release before he went to join his ancestors. A sort of twist to the usual Shinto bit about ritual washing.

You mean that he meant to try again, said the doctor.

No, said Cadbury. He was waiting for his *kaishaku*. Now let's go and look at the bloody remains.

They finished their coffee in silence.

The policeman at the door was in a terrible state. He had sworn already that no one could possibly have got past without him noticing.

Not even me, said Cadbury as she posed provocatively with one hand on her hip.

It's all right, Juan, said Ritornello, with his hand on the

man's shoulder. There are dozens of nurses, and we didn't tell you to stop any. Or anyone else, for that matter. You were there to keep the bastard in, and stop him finding a weapon.

So it was her, said the policeman, looking in awe at Cadbury.

As far as we know, no, said Piangi. But she'd like to be on the list of suspects.

I'll wait here, said the policeman. I've seen him once already.

He must have come in through the window, said Piangi as they skirted the bed. There are marks on the woodwork, and I'm sure we'll find footprints outside. It must have been easy enough to leg over the sill and do the job in no time.

My God, said Cadbury.

The body of the Japanese lay face down on the floor beside the bed. He had apparently been sitting cross-legged, and his torso had fallen forward over his knees with the force of the blow from behind. The stump of his neck had been covered with a white cloth, now soaked red with his blood. A yard away on the floor his severed head lay grotesquely askew, with the open eyes on the door. The expression was calm, and the mouth closed. There was no sign of a weapon.

He must have risen from the bed, said the doctor, and knelt down as you see him. Perhaps to pray, or to do some exercise. He would have had his back to the window, and the murderer could have come up behind him and stood here.

The doctor took up a position at the corner of the bed.

He would have taken a long swing with his weapon, whatever it was, brought it down across the neck bone and cut right through the flesh and bone. The head would naturally have rolled away and come to rest about where you see it.

Unless it was all moved, said Cadbury.

You can see it wasn't moved, said the doctor. There's no blood on the bed. As I said before, he added irritably.

So he was forced to rise and sit down cross-legged with his back to the window. And wait to be killed, said Piangi. I wonder he didn't take a risk and yell for help.

He wasn't forced, said Cadbury.

The point is, she explained when they sat alone together in the doctor's office a little later, that he expected to be killed, and wanted to be.

The doctor had gone on his morning rounds, and she felt able to speak more freely.

Tell me more about the old nurse in Paris, said Piangi. He fingered her knee, as if he was genuinely interested.

I told you, the carriage was empty. She made me stand with my back against the metal support beside the door.

She made you?

I mean I wanted to by then. My school skirt was pretty short, and I had on these navy-blue knickers. If it makes you stiff, she added, you can reach behind my knees. But keep your hands at least a foot from my crutch.

They were sitting facing each other, in full view of the window. Cadbury heeled her shoe off and lifted her leg so that her left foot lay in Ritornello's lap. His nails crackled as he stroked the mesh of her tights.

She stood in front of me, said Cadbury, with her cape open. Her dress had horn buttons down the front, and she undid them below the waist. I remember she had a pretty cunty smell, and her breath was awful. She was wearing an iron ring.

Piangi had stopped stroking behind her knees. He put both hands to his waist and undid his tweed trousers. Underneath he was wearing white Y-fronted underpants. Cadbury reached forward with her toes and flexed them gently into the slit.

She reached under my skirt, said Cadbury, and tugged my knickers halfway down my thighs. They just caught in the tops of my garters. Then she took hold of her own pants and pulled them away to one side. They were made of a sort of frilly lace, I remember. The metal support of the door felt icy-cold on my bottom. I could taste the stale soot from the tunnels when I swallowed.

Outside the window, a pair of young nurses went past laughing and talking. Cadbury leaned over her shoulder and formed her lips into a kiss for one. She was a dark girl with full, heavy breasts, and she smiled back. She didn't seem to see what Cadbury was doing to Piangi.

If you want them to see, said Cadbury in a soft voice, you'd better take it out.

She lifted and bent her leg back, allowing her skirt to fall high up on her thighs. Piangi licked his lips. His hands moved of their own accord to ease himself through the tight cotton.

What a manly man you are, said Cadbury.

She put out her leg again and allowed her toes to run up and down what was now on full view to the passing nurses in the courtyard. There were sounds of laughter and giggling as Piangi sat with his eyes clenched shut.

What happened next, he asked hoarsely.

She reached her coarse old hands under my buttocks and forced me hard against her. The ring was grinding into my flesh from behind. The way she pushed, the lips of my vulva came right forward, and she started to rotate her cunt in a sort of lunging way so that she brushed regularly along mine. We were both pretty wet by then, and I soon got the knack of how to help. I remember the swishy sound and the cool feel of those lace knickers she had.

While Cadbury spoke, she allowed her voice to grow deeper and softer. Her toes clutched and moved in their slippery nylon, and Piangi sat with his knees apart and the whole middle of his body concentrated in her delicate pattern of tensions and pressures. Outside, a little group of nurses had paused. They pretended to chatter among themselves, watching covertly what was happening to the man in the room.

So after a while I was on the edge, said Cadbury as her foot paused in its work. We were nearly at the terminal and I knew she was going to try to bring me off at the exact moment the train came to a stop. I could hardly move, with my knickers holding my legs, and she wouldn't allow me to slip them down. I just had to stand still and enjoy it. I was absolutely her mistress.

The dark girl in the group at the window had turned, and was frankly staring in. Her eyes looked at Cadbury, and Cadbury held them with a slow stare directly on her own. She lifted her leg from Piangi's body, and bent it in the air, so that the dark girl could look up and along it to her groin.

And then we shuddered to a halt in the darkness. And I came, half kneeling on her.

Cadbury's leg swung back, and she clutched and ran her toes in a series of quick rhythmic movements along the throbbing stiffness Piangi could no more control than the tides or the moon. Her eyes fixed on the girl outside the window, watching fascinated as the man's sperm began to jet and spurt into his cupped hands. The girl stood with her lips parted, blushing, and then turned and ran across the courtyard.

You see, she enjoyed it, said Cadbury. We all do.

The other nurses had gone, and the yard was empty. Piangi had done his trousers up, and washed his hands.

You do it to humiliate, he said.

I do it to please, said Cadbury. And to educate.

Explain.

You were so sexed up you could think of nothing else. I need your attention, and your respect. So I had to help you out. And fairly fast.

In front of the window. With all those girls.

You knew they were there, said Cadbury. And it turned you on. That's education, mate. And the power bit about it turned *me* on. If I don't enjoy it myself, I never do anything well. And it takes a lot of skill and lust to use your toes like that.

So you had an orgasm, said Piangi, lighting another Caporal and leaning back in his chair.

I didn't need one. You did.

Piangi smiled.

I like you, Cadbury, he said.

It was murder by consent, said Cadbury a few moments later as they walked together back to Piangi's car. When a

Japanese arranges to kill himself, he normally has a sort of second, or *kaishaku,* present to give him the *coup de grâce.* The job of this other lad is to chop his head off with a single stroke of a full-length samurai sword, or *katana,* after he's got the whole thing off to a good start by slitting his belly open with a little dagger called a *tanto.* Usually, of course, this all takes place within a space of a few minutes.

They had paused and were looking out across the bay towards the oil-cracking plant at La Linea. The flame that never went out by night or day was burning on its pillar. A breath of wind caught and blew it into a whirlwind of strange shapes in the air.

But on this occasion, said Cadbury, it required a total of nearly four days. Poor bugger. I wonder what he was thinking about.

Tadashi Soko, said Piangi as they watched the wind furrow the water. Aged fifty. Dealer in antiquities, according to the translation we have of his passport designation. Soldier in Burma, no doubt, or in the Philippines. A man like myself. And yet I couldn't do what he did.

I wonder, said Cadbury. If only we had the imagination to see the sexuality of violence. . . . It might make it easier.

Piangi unlocked the door of the car. A gust of wind caught him and blew his sparse hair about.

So who was his accomplice, he said.

The one who took the sword from the case at the school, said Cadbury. The one who used it, I think, to kill him with. The one who drives a Datsun very fast, and nearly crashed with my taxi on the way to London airport. It has to be him.

She looked up at Piangi and smiled.

The one whom I am going to pick up and swim with

this morning at Catalan Bay. A bastard. And a Japanese.

Do you want a lift to the Rock, said Piangi.

Cadbury kissed his cheek.

It has to be him and not you, she said, because it's the best way to meet them and not arouse suspicion. No normal man on his own on an airplane can ignore an apparently totally wanton and unaccompanied woman. Particularly if all that she seems to need is sex. He marks her down as an object. A body without a mind. And when he sees her again, he wants the sex rather more than the first time. Because it isn't so easy to get in that pure form, without money and without complications. And he's all ripe for the plucking. A sucker. Who can't see that a girl can use her sex like a man can use his gun. To exploit and subvert. And so he goes under. As this one is going to.

And all you get for your pains is a good fuck, said Piangi.

It comes to that, said Cadbury. Will you drop me here?

And she ran up the sloping ramp past the palm trees to the door of the Rock. Somewhere a church clock was chiming ten, the hour of the snake.

The Hour of the Snake

10:00 A.M.

7

The young Japanese was finishing his breakfast. Outside the window of his bedroom at the Caleta Palace Hotel, the wind was lifting the gray surface of the Mediterranean into long ruffles topped with spume. But the sun was shining, and a few guests had already come out with towels and dark glasses onto the roof of the terrace. The Japanese watched them idly as he swallowed the last piece of toast and marmalade. Like his emperor, he had learned to enjoy the full excesses of the British morning ritual, and had ordered a tray of eggs, bacon, sausages, and tomato. The girl who had brought them had seemed surprised. Her mental image of the Japanese breakfast had been of something more exotic and less substantial.

Yamaka Tsukamoto drank the remains of his coffee and leaned back in the black swivel chair, which was the only piece of furniture in this anonymous room he could tolerate. He looked around with distaste at the light-salmon pastel shade of the walls, the eighteenth-century prints of the siege, the pale unpainted softwood of the furnishings. By English standards they were cool and elegant, in a tasteful and modern way. To his eye, they were barren and cluttered at once, the cowardly bargain a decadent empire had made with the heirs of William Morris. He let his eyes wander again to the window, across the empty plain of the sea towards the East, and then down to the handful of people in swimsuits beginning to drape themselves on the ten or eleven deck chairs in the sun.

He was partly dressed in traditional Japanese style. A loose gray kimono hung around his shoulders, and he wore a broad silk sash tightly wound at his waist. The hilt of a short sword protruded from the sash at his left side, and there were wooden raised sandals on his feet. The kimono was of strong, rough silk, and a single mon, the three inward-facing leaves of the wild ginger plant, the crest of the Tokugawa clan, was patterned in skillful embroidery on the back and on each shoulder. It was a crest much misused, and Yamaka's lips had often curled in scorn to see it on cheap lacquer saké cups, and even wash cloths. But there was a reason why he and his friends had sworn to wear it. It was the symbol for the ordered Society of Tokugawa Ieyasu, where everything had its place and the barbarians were only admitted with their trinkets to the Dutch trading post at Nagasaki.

Yamaka stretched his arms, and reached behind him for the golf bag that lay on the bed. He caught it by the shoulder strap and hauled it over to his lap. Unbuttoning the side pocket, where the balls were kept, he took out an oilskin envelope bound with a cord. He untied the cord and laid out the envelope and its contents along the bedspread. An observer might well have assumed they were tools for the maintenance of a small car or bicycle. There were files, what looked like a screwdriver, a small silver hammer, tubes of oil and grease, some colored twine, a measuring tape, and a set of brushes. There was also a small bag with a handle, and a packet of tissues.

As he spread and fingered these tools in their places on the oilskin, Yamaka was aware of the people on the terrace settling for their morning sun. They were chatting together, or spreading their long or heavy bodies on the warming covering of the sun chairs. He grimaced at the horror of ill-kept British flesh as he pushed the bag away and rose to his feet. He walked to the bedroom door and turned the key on the inside to lock it. Returning to the bed, he hoisted up the golf bag, unfastened the main flap, and drew something from the inside. He poised it for a moment in his bare hands, then pressed it briefly against his forehead.

The object of this attention, which he now laid on the bed, was a long, slightly curved piece of unpainted shaped wood, without pattern and without projections. A close examination would have revealed only two breaks in the completely even flow of the lines: a small circular wooden peg about three inches from one end, which seemed to go right through the wood, and was flush with the surface at each point of exit, and a thin tight line, as of two sections meeting at a point, about seven inches from the same end of the object.

A student of Japanese weapons would have recognized it as a good-quality *shirazaya,* the plain scabbard of white magnolia wood in which the samurai was wont to preserve his swords when not in use for battle or display. From this *shirazaya,* Yamaka now drew out with long and sensuous care the exquisite gleaming curved steel of a beautifully made *katana.* The blade flashed when the sun caught it, and the wavy line of the *yakiba* met and aligned itself with the shimmer of the clouds along the horizon. Below its gray sweep, the sunburned flesh of the English tourists seemed to contract and pulsate with a kind of anticipatory shiver of horror, as if the wind of retribution had blown with a sudden icy gust from the East. Yamaka smiled as he watched them strip and posture, their swollen bellies bulging over the flowered trunks and wet-look bras. He allowed the edge of the blade to drop a little, so that it seemed for a moment to sever the head of a fat, bald man with a handkerchief on his face. He smiled again, and reached down to the envelope for a tissue. The surface of the blade was sticky with drying blood.

While he wiped the blade with the tissue, Yamaka remembered how the man had died. There had been no time for the usual rituals, the farewells and formulas of traditional seppuku. He had swung in through the window with the *shirazaya,* and given Tadashi Soko the Benzedrine. No words had passed between them. Tadashi had been ready. With the aid of the drug, he had risen of his own accord and seated himself beside the bed for a brief moment of prayer and meditation. Yamaka had taken the risk of counting ten, and had cut him down with the *hassenmaki,* as executioners had done with the bodies of criminals. He had not worn the right clothes, and he had not had time to arrange the body or to clean the sword. He had sheathed it in the wooden scabbard, swung his leg over the sill, and left the hospital the way he had come, as a tourist with an unusual walking stick. It had taken him only twenty minutes to drive the short journey around the Rock to Catalan Bay, and a late breakfast in his room after an early-morning walk had surprised no one.

He examined the blade now in the light as he dropped the bloody tissue into the wastebasket. There was scarcely a mark on the flowing steel. He tilted the blade so that the gleaming outline of his face was visible in the burnished mirror-surface of the *shinogi* behind the hard steel of the edge. He tilted it again, and enjoyed the misty blur of his features in the unpolished metal of the *jigane* as it flowed towards the *hamon*. In the quivering miracle of the *yakiba*, he began to feel the dream of the perfect islands in the water when Izenagi shook them for the first time from the point of his spear. The edge flowed on its own, without flaw or *chizu*, an invisible boundary between the living and the dead, separated forever, as they should be, by the cold laws of *Bushido*.

On the terrace below the window, the bald man lay supine, with his hairy belly rising and falling irregularly when he breathed. A scrawny woman in a straw hat had allowed her skirt to ride up over her knees, and a blotchy waste of flesh stretched out on the towel spread below her. Yamaka winced, and allowed the sword again to swoop and remove her legs in the traditional cut of the *rio kuruma*.

Die, he said. You have no *kami*. No spirit.

He lifted the small bag from the oilskin and allowed its soft bulge to stroke the surface of the blade. A white powder leaked out and dusted the gleaming metal. With another tissue, he wiped away the *Wiener Kalk* and returned the *uchiko* to its place. From a thin tube he squeezed out a layer of oil. It smelled slightly of cloves. With another tissue he spread it gently all over the flowing lines and ridges of the weapon so that it was completely coated with a thin, almost invisible film.

As he finished this operation, Yamaka lifted the blade again. He admired the single long groove on the ridge, like the furrow of the first plow in the dawn of Hokkaido. He let his eye sink in the complex *katakiri* engraving where it flowered into a coiling dragon's body around a spear just above the tang. There was something unearthly and remote about it now, the dream of a samurai for the perfect sword. He swung it again, as if for the famous *O-kesa* cut that would sever a man in two pieces from the waist to the shoulder.

Holding the sword in the air, Yamaka removed his left hand from the hilt and reached once more into the long pocket of the golf bag. He drew out the slender curving shape of a decorated lacquer scabbard, of the same size and shape as the *shirazaya*. With an easy relaxed movement, as if allowing a falcon to return to its perch, he returned the sword of Yasutsuna to its formal residence, the beautiful patterned scabbard of white *same-nuri* in which it had lain for centuries.

Outside, a new guest had arrived on the sun terrace among the grotesque array of the old and the overfed. She shook her long yellow hair over her bare shoulders as she looked about for a vacant sun chair to lie on. Yamaka smiled when he saw her. He slid the wooden peg from the hilt of the sword and eased off the wooden *tsuka*. The cold unworked steel of the tang lay in his palm, and he allowed his finger to play over the two characters for Yasutsuna which the smith had hammered with his beautiful free strokes into the metal over a thousand years before.

As he stroked the coolness of the tiny grooves, the girl

walked over to a free place and rolled her bright crimson towel as a cushion for her head. She stretched her long body full length on the hot plastic and rolled over onto her belly.

Yamaka turned away from the window again for a moment and drew something else from the side pocket of the golf bag. It was an embroidered brocade bag, tied with a silk cord. Slipping the cord aside, he watched the girl on the terrace arrange her limbs in a comfortable position. She flexed the muscles of her stomach, as if to bring as much of herself as possible in contact with the hot surface she was lying on.

From the bag Yamaka shook out six pieces of wood and metal onto the bedspread. With his thumb and forefinger he picked up one of these and slid it neatly over the end of the tang, thrusting it down until it fitted exactly and snugly over the tuck at the juncture of the tang and the blade. The piece was a broad metal sheath, or holder, roughly engraved with file marks.

With this ring, I thee wed, said Yamaka to himself.

The girl squirmed as if something had bitten or dug into her. She reached a hand behind her back and scratched the plump flesh just above the right buttock-piece of her swimsuit.

Yamaka had slid another piece of metal over the tang. The small copper oval with the milled edge and the coffin shape of the blade section cut through it slipped into position with a faint metal chink. He covered it with his fingers and slipped on the broad, heavy *mokko* shape of the iron guard, with its indentation of hammered pawlonia flowers. It lay on the first *seppa*, Yamaka thought, like an old samurai as he covers a young virgin for the first time.

Outside the window, the girl pressed her body along the chair. Her legs flexed at the knee, and she lifted one in the air, allowing her toes to knead the air.

Yamaka slid on the second *seppa,* and enjoyed the satisfying chink as it closed along the top side of the *tsuba.* He imagined the old warrior surprised from behind when the second virgin slid in against his buttocks.

The girl lowered her leg and seemed to wriggle. She reached both hands behind her back and rolled down the elastic top of her swimsuit pants, lowering the material along her bottom to reveal a broader expanse of white buttocks to the now warmer lash of the sunlight.

Yamaka paused in his work. His eyes slithered in a kind of abstract pleasure over the body of this girl he had first noticed in the Trident two days ago. He was looking forward to a swim with her.

The girl wriggled again. She was easing the pants out from under her. While Yamaka watched, they cleared the peaks of her buttocks and laid bare the deep dark valley filled with hair in between them. In spite of himself, he began to feel an excitement. When his gaze took in that furry aperture, he could almost believe her to be a naked, wanton boy, with his huge firm prick thrusting down for relief into some unseen hole or cavity in the chair. He felt himself harden with lust as he quickened his mounting of the sword.

With trembling fingers he fitted the *fuchi* over the wooden projection of the hilt, allowing his fingers to flicker on the twined cord over the *menuki* against the rayskin. It took only a quick thrust, and a hard slap, to bring the whole apparatus firmly in place along the tang, as tight and close as a hand-made contraceptive sheath for a shogun's emissary. Slipping the wooden pin in place was the work of a moment.

The girl lay still and lax, her plump thighs now spread apart, her pants half down. As he watched, she lifted both arms above her head and stretched them limply along the edge of the seat, so that the rough black hair under her armpits was bared. It was more than Yamaka could stand. She lay spread-eagled like the boy playing Jesus in a male brothel he had once visited in Paris, when three men had used him, one between the cheeks of his anus and one under each of his arms. He opened the sash of his kimono and stood upright at the window, the stiff arch of his male organ unveiled and visible in the sun.

Behind him, on the bed, the sword of Yasutsuna lay asleep in its own scabbard, satisfied an hour earlier by the orgasm of blood in the death of Tadashi Soko at the General Hospital. The hour of the snake was over.

8

The man's long body arrowed into the gray water with only the slightest disturbance when he plunged from the flat diving rock above the sea pool. Cadbury trod water by the jagged half-submerged rocks and watched as his sleek head resurfaced, shook itself, and turned towards her. Drops formed on the taut skin of his forehead as he blinked, arched over on his back, and dived like a seal out of sight. Seconds later she felt the slide of his cold hands up her thighs, and his mouth pressed for a moment against the soaked, close nylon of her pants before his face re-emerged and his powerful hairy arms were drawing him back on the splashed rocks. He leaned and kicked water up, his eyes appraising her quizzically.

I bet you were watching me from the window, said Cadbury.

You left me exhausted. We shall have to confine ourselves to a swim and some coffee.

Sex maniac, said Cadbury, and she struck out towards the open sea with a fluid, easy breast stroke.

The man watched the tightening of the muscles in her back and the rounded hump of her bottom as she surged away from him. Her long hair was out of sight under a smooth rubber bathing cap, and except for the thin black line of her bra strap across her back, it might have been the lithe body of a boy he was watching ease itself through the water. He felt a new excitement, and flung himself savagely forward again into the sea. With a swift, clawing free crawl, he had covered the twenty yards between himself and the girl in a few seconds, rolled over on his side, and begun to haul himself hard away in front of her with an even faster free back stroke.

As he drew farther ahead in a white flurry of spume kicked up by his driving heels, Cadbury increased the speed of her even breast stroke. She kept her head above water and watched him extend his lead. He was fast, but she knew she could catch him. She began to dip her head with each stroke, driving her body forward with a series of long, rhythmic swoops. When the man reached the rock he had been aiming for, which marked the gap between the pool and the open sea, she had cut the distance by several yards.

You're faster than I thought, he said, pushing the long hair from his eyes.

You were showing off, she said.

For a woman, you swim well. But speed is a man's business.

As when you're driving out to London airport.

For example, said Yamaka.

He turned and threw himself fast and hard through the gap in the rocks, beating with his furious crawl into the heavy swell of waves that were coming for Gibraltar all the way from the toe of Italy. He became a white swirl of spray, a dwindling ball in the water, while Cadbury lay back on the cutting edge of the limestone and watched him go. He was like her Ferrari, she reflected, always anxious to have its throttle opened on a piece of clear road.

You Japanese bastard, she said. You're not a man, you're a machine.

Yamaka had turned, and his white aureole of spume was again increasing in size as he flung himself back to where she was waiting. When he drew level, and paused, treading water, she took a deep breath, dived, and with a powerful scissor-twitch of her legs, plunged underneath him, turned and slid her hands from below over the firm bulge in his trunks.

I'll race you to the shore, she said as she slithered away with a quick side stroke to the far rocks.

On your mark, woman, he replied.

So Cadbury went into her own fast crawl, and was yards away before he had started. He would let her get well ahead, then aim to catch up, surge in front, and win by a few close strokes. Turn to congratulate her. Then kiss her on the mouth, breathless as she would be. And carry her off indoors to do what he would with her in his room. Only it wasn't going to be like that. He was tired from showing off, by the loss of his sperm, and in reaction to his early-morning bloodletting. And he wouldn't admit this to himself.

Cadbury felt the sudden flurry in the water as Yamaka began to come up alongside. Her eyes opened as she drove forward, and she saw the cream blur of his threshing body, halved by the black rippling powerhouse of his trunks. She could sense the total energy of his effort as he moved in the water. He had calculated on her being at full stretch, and he was going flat out. There were still ten yards to the rocks at the shore when Yamaka began to pass her. The black squelch of his flailing trunks broke level with her eyes as Cadbury jammed her heart into overdrive. Her stroke changed for a second into a huge, double overhand butterfly as she arched and wheeled in a tremendous orgasmic burst of female force and calculation towards the shore. It was like giving birth. Her hands closed on the wet slippery limestone, and she emptied herself into a climax of panting as Yamaka's clenched fist leaped and struck at the cutting rock only a yard behind her.

There was a long silence while they hung on the rocks, gasping uncontrollably for air. The cold wind furrowed the sea as the salt and sweat began to dry on their heaving skin. Blood coursed in Yamaka's cut hand, and he wiped it roughly across the hair on his chest. Water ran on the bones of his cheeks like rain on a window. He said something softly to himself in Japanese.

Never underestimate a woman, breathed Cadbury, tilting her head back to look up at the sky.

You tricked me, Yamaka said. For half the way I let you win. You were faster than I thought.

You said that before, said Cadbury as she leaned her head on his chest.

Yamaka looked down at the soft light hair on her neck. She lay against him like a boy he was teaching to swim. The little hard buttocks in their close pants. The coiled worm at the front he could so easily reach down and quicken with his fingers. He tried to forget the voluptuous sweep of those proud breasts above the rib cage.

Let's go inside, he said.

He hauled himself from the water onto the rocks. The sea flowed off his long body, and he stood dripping, with his hand extended to help her up. She could feel the strength still in his arm as he drew her easily to her feet, and they walked together towards the hotel.

In the bathroom of Yamaka's suite, Cadbury directed the flowering jets of nearly scalding water from the shower nozzle against the erogenous zones around her nipples and below her pelvic girdle. Things were going to be difficult. This particular Japanese was a man whose life was ruled by competition. It was important to him to win, and he usually succeeded in doing so.

Which is why, she reflected as she directed the shower under her armpits, he is now going to be feeling more than a little shaken up. And in need of further reassurance.

Has the coffee come, she called through the closed door.

It has. Please hurry up, he replied.

He sounded cold and remote. Stepping from the hip bath in a haze of steam, Cadbury ran over the situation as she currently saw it. Her telephone call to the Caleta Palace last night, and her subsequent discovery, as she had expected, that there was only one Japanese in residence. A Mr. Yamaka Tsukamoto.

Who has only this morning used a ceremonial sword in the act of decapitation, she thought as she started to towel the moisture from her skin. Let us hope that he needs to boast about this to his now a little more mysteriously competitive girl friend.

She reached up for the yellow ball on the glass shelf, which she had already noticed and been amused by before her shower.

I never thought they used it themselves, she said to herself, dabbing powder from the ball onto the fluffy yellow puff and beginning to apply it to her ears and her eyelashes, and then lightly over the ticklish soles of her feet as she squatted on the cork top of the bath-side seat.

And then she remembered that *kiku* was the Japanese for chrysanthemum, the crest of the Imperial family.

As Cadbury walked through into the bedroom, dry and stark naked, Yamaka was looking out the window. He was standing with his back to her, and said without looking around:

Come over here, please.

She walked obediently towards him and stood with her hands at her sides. Yamaka turned and took hold of her long hair in both hands. He was holding a gray slubbed-silk scarf, and he used this to knot and hold her hair in a coiled mass on top of her head.

That's better, he said. Now put this on.

He pointed to a black silk kimono on the bed, and watched as she slipped her arms into it and drew it around her body. It was small, and fitted well. It felt cool on her skin. Yamaka eyed her appreciatively.

Now put the sash on, he said.

As Cadbury drew the kimono close and fastened the obi around her waist, Yamaka reached into a drawer in the dressing table and took out something long and narrow from a brocade bag. He unloosened the cord that held it and drew something out, which he came over and tucked in her sash. She dropped her fingers to it, feeling the cold metal *kashira* and then the bulging silk twine of a sword hilt.

What on earth is this for, she said. Are we playing charades? Or is it a little Noh play in reverse, where the men's parts are played by women?

You have a little penis of your own now, said Yamaka softly. Just like a boy. A very very pretty little boy.

So that's it, thought Cadbury. She had already begun to suspect as much in the pool. Sweet Loyola, be with me now, she thought. I shall have a special new turn-on for you tomorrow. Were you in the army, she said aloud.

I was too young, boy, said Yamaka. My brother was a kamikaze. I was old enough to drink saké with him before his flight. I helped bind the flowers on his flying helmet. Some plum blossom, and a little lespedeza.

As they sat on the bed together a few minutes later, the tears began to dry from Yamaka's eyes.

I was about your age, boy, he said. Will there ever be another chance to wipe out the shame?

He reached behind him for the golf bag on the floor, slid up the flap, and drew out the long sword of Yasutsuna in its mottled scabbard of *same-nuri*. With an easy movement, he swung out the blade and made it arc in the warm air, catching the sun rising as it broke through the window.

Be careful, said Cadbury. You could cut someone's head off with a thing like that.

It has already cut many heads off, said Yamaka, without emotion. You see the skin wrapped around the magnolia wood of the *tsuka*, boy. It is the skin of the sting ray. We choose it because it looks like a crust of pearls. And because the ray will strike like the lash of a sword. Here in your old imperial island I remember Lord Nelson, and how he whipped the French in 1805. A hundred years later our Admiral Togo smashed the Russian fleet in Tsushima Bay. My grandfather was there. He wore that little *tanto* in your belt. You beat me in the sea. So wear it.

Where did the long sword come from, said Cadbury, reaching her hand out as if to fondle the glittering steel.

Never touch the blade, said Yamaka, stopping her. Your moisture soils it with rust. And it brings bad luck. Or it would if you were a woman, boy, he added as he pushed her so she fell away from him on the bed with her breasts out of sight.

Did that belong to your grandfather, too, said Cadbury.

It belongs to me, said Yamaka as he became aware again of the vulnerable dip in her shoulders. Or, rather, it belongs to us. To the samurai of Japan.

Put it back for a while in its sheath, said Cadbury.

She turned over to kneel with her face in the pillow, pushing her buttocks gently through the kimono against Yamaka's hip.

It wants to come back in its sheath, said Cadbury softly. Back in its sheath.

She heard the muffled clatter as the precious blade fell

away from Yamaka's hand to the floor. She reached down into the side pocket of the golf bag and pulled out the leather envelope. Her fingers began to unlace it as her bottom pressed and rolled slightly against Yamaka's rigid leg.

I wonder what's in here, she said while she spread and fingered the tools.

Her buttocks began to work with a heavier rhythm as Yamaka swung himself on the bed behind her. He crouched and stared at the long swoop of her neck, the bared ears and the tight-combed samurai hair. The hilt of the short sword stuck up from beneath her, provoking and military in its savage beauty. He began to stroke the engraved decoration in gold on *shakudo nanako,* the armor of the two generals at the river. He could feel his own sword firm in the tight scabbard of his half-dry trunks below his kimono. He reached forward and raised the boy's kimono slowly over the silky muscles of his thighs, dusting the soft hairs on the backs of the buttocks as he eased it up to his waist and laid it along his back. The passage of his desire was rough and ready for him. He forced his way forward, his left hand fingering the stiff hilt of the *tanto* in its sheath.

My Christ, thought Cadbury when she felt the indecent half-exciting pressure begin. Has the bastard never heard of *vaseline?*

She lay with her mind working at whatever erotic images she could summon, aware only of the man's dreaming male action at the cheeks of her rectum, his need to feel her entirely a virgin boy. Despite herself, a gasping squeal was torn from her lips as a particularly fierce thrust seemed about to burst her poor body in two halves like an apple ripped by a chimpanzee.

Yamaka grew more excited. The boy was in pain. And yet he could bear it. The poor, beautiful boy. He would force him until he screamed, and then caress his injured anus with the sweetest and coolest creams and ointments. And take his prick in his fingers. He lunged again.

As the raw agony began to tear at the self-control she was still fighting to hold herself in, Cadbury began to clutch for strength at the tools in the leather envelope. Her hands closed over the silver hammer, the long brushes, the soft powdery ball of the *uchiko*. As if for comfort, she thrust the tight wad of it firmly into her lips, biting and inhaling as the last berserk strokes of the man on her back began to forge to their climax.

She felt a sudden burning sensation in her nose, a strange intense smell, and then the upsurge of a blinding joy as the powerful thrusts began to dig to their final depth. She squirmed with a real delight, rotating her buttocks in a fierce access of hungry desire when Yamaka began to explode in the throes of his orgasm.

You little bugger, You beautiful little bugger, he gasped as he lay heaving for breath along Cadbury's half-stripped body, sweating and still erect when she turned below him.

Close your eyes, you bastard, she said.

As she stroked his lashes down, she ripped her kimono apart, pulling off the obi and allowing the sword to fall aside. Heaving herself up, she pushed Yamaka down on his back, straddled him, and grasped his oily prick in her two hands. In the blinding excitement that shot hot spasms through her rocketing brain, she drove him deep inside her and rode his body like a man killing his last horse in a desperate relay race. She came somehow—she never knew when—as Yamaka rolled her off onto the floor and spat with revulsion on her breasts.

The drug continued to work in her head while she lay recovering on the carpet, and Yamaka washed, at length and with care, in the bathroom. And underneath its white explosion, she began to put another piece of the puzzle into place.

The Hour of the Horse

12:00 NOON

9

It was fifteen minutes to twelve. There was an air of expectancy in the sun lounge of the Rock Hotel. Guests were standing or sitting about in small groups, talking or drinking cocktails. From where Cadbury sat in her high-backed basket chair, she had a good view over the damaged tops of the palm trees towards the swimming pool. A boy was clearing a drift of leaves from the water with a long stick. It had been a rough night. The wind had fallen, but the effects of its ferocity were to be seen everywhere.

Bianco. With ice and lemon, said a voice at Cadbury's elbow. It might be a description of the lady herself.

Cadbury looked up from her drink. The steward from the flight out was smiling down at her.

Are you all alone?

You're never alone with a *Penthouse,* said Cadbury as she tapped the magazine in her lap.

Strange company, said the steward. The same again?

Cadbury nodded while he gestured to the waiter. The arrival of the steward was not unwelcome. The Trident was due in a few minutes, and a chaperone through the barrier could turn out to be useful. Since leaving Yamaka the previous afternoon, she had spoken at length to Valerian on the telephone, and it was clear that a rapid return to London was essential. Unfortunately, the open line had not allowed her to explain her discovery in detail.

There wasn't much room in the bag, she had said. I suppose a few pounds of *kiku*. But it really smelled very strange.

You'd better come home, said Valerian. I hardly trust you on those exotic beaches.

You needn't worry, said Cadbury. The wind is rising. And I never look my best in goose pimples.

The wind had risen with a vengeance. As she lay awake in her white room on the sea side of the hotel, she had heard it howl and moan whenever it rattled a loose shutter on the screen of her balcony. She had twice tumbled sleepily out of bed to close it, and on each occasion the storm had seemed to increase in violence. Doors had slammed far off in the corridors, and she had fallen uneasily asleep to dream of catastrophes with swords and bloodshed.

At breakfast, she had seen something of the night's damage through the hotel window. Across the road a light sports car had been flung heavily against a lamp post and lay with its offside fender smashed in and useless. Branches had been swept away from the palm trees in the garden and blocked the drive with a chaos of ferny green.

The paper says it's the worst weather for ten years, the boy who served her breakfast had said.

Cadbury had sipped her coffee, watching the white spume scudding over the metal of the sea. Fishing boats had been rocking at anchor, and she remembered the bustle on the deck of the submarine. It had looked as if they were having difficulty in preparing to put to sea. But there were more urgent problems on her mind.

She was virtually certain that the white powder in Ya-maka's *uchiko* had not been chalk. It had been something considerably more valuable.

The waiter brought the drinks, and Cadbury watched as the steward paid.

She made a sudden decision.

May I ask you about this crime story I'm reading, she said.

Fire away, said the steward.

There's this couple of thieves, said Cadbury, with a carefully assumed eager seriousness. They steal swords. All sorts of swords. Big swords and little swords. Viking swords and little Polynesian daggers. Apparently just for their own sake—I mean, to make money by selling them. And they smuggle them out of the British Isles.

You mean by sea.

I mean by airplane, said Cadbury.

It's not so easy, said the steward.

And for several minutes, exactly as Cadbury had wanted him to, he elaborated on the security precautions at London airport, and the complex regulations affecting the handling and export of weapons.

Most of the other guests had drifted away into the main lobby of the hotel. The few left were looking anxious, and consulting their watches. The plane was late. They fidgeted with the locks of their suitcases, checked to make sure they had their tickets and passports with them, engaged the representatives of the airline in endless speculative conversation.

It's left Tangier, said one of these reassuringly. It can't be many minutes more. We shall leave in the bus as soon as we see it come in to land.

Cadbury watched the wind whipping the waves into jagged white crests. She felt a tinge of worry. She was fairly sure that Yamaka had no suspicions, but the telephone call to Valerian had been a risk. And it might have had consequences. She would feel a lot happier the sooner she was safely back in London. She concentrated, and continued to listen to the steward.

I know, she said when he reached the end of his complex and invaluable explanations. That's just the point. And you've confirmed it, as I hoped you would. You see they take advantage of all those regulations to cover up their real concerns. They're not, as it turns out, sword thieves at all. All the swords they steal and smuggle out are just a cover. What they're really smuggling is cocaine.

Cadbury paused for effect.

Once in a while, she continued, they even mean to get caught with their swords, to keep the regulations tough. Then they start on their real business. They begin to work with dealers. Men with perfectly respectable businesses in the buying and selling of swords. And they declare and expose all the weapons they move to and fro. And, of course, nobody is in the least interested. A sword you can see is no longer a threat. They turn them over to the stewards at the beginning of flights, and they get them back at the end. It's the perfect cover, it's so legitimate. And inside the scabbards and the cleaning kits for the swords, in the brocade bags they preserve them in, there's always plenty of preservative oil. And chalk to dust it down with.

Cadbury paused dramatically, and sipped her drink.

Only this chalk, she went on. This white powder we call chalk. Is really cocaine. Thousands and thousands of pounds of smuggled cocaine. I thought it was really quite a clever plot, she finished, with a smile. What do *you* think?

It's coming now, said a voice from the lobby.

Cadbury turned in her chair. She could see a tiny shape in the sky above the point. She rose and walked to the window, standing to look out with the steward beside her. The shape had grown wings and was taking on the peculiar high-tailed look of a Trident. As Cadbury watched, the pilot brought it around the end of the island and down towards the strip at La Linea.

There was a buzz of excited talk, and the guests all lined the windows, pointing and laughing. The white crests ran in long lines on the water, and the flame flickered wildly above the oil-cracking plant.

He's coming in low, said the steward. Must be the wind.

The Trident seemed to hang for a long time without moving, a silver flaw in the enormous wind-washed canvas of the Algeciras sky. Slowly, it crept in a level line from left to right across the hotel's plate-glass windows.

Cadbury felt her mouth grow dry. She crossed her legs at the ankles, resisting a sudden desire to go to the lavatory. She must wait and see it land first.

They don't very often come in as low as that, said the steward, his eyes fixed on the line of the wings.

The Trident was closing on the landing strip.

He has to lower his nose at exactly the right moment, the steward explained. The strip, as you know, goes across the peninsula from sea to sea. So he can't afford to undershoot.

Or he's in the ditch. And if he overshoots, he has to go around again. If he has the fuel. It's a tricky job.

The Trident's nose began to drop for the final run. There was a sigh of relief from the watching faces. Cadbury's palms were moist, and she felt the desire to evacuate herself growing stronger and stronger between her legs. She fought back the movement in her bowels with a tight clasping of her thighs.

Just right, said the steward. Pretty bloody well perfect in these conditions, I'd say.

As he spoke, the Trident seemed suddenly to falter. The downward droop of its nose wavered, then sharply changed. For no reason the watchers in the hotel could see, the plane banked and rose, turning away from the strip towards La Linea.

My God, said the steward. He's balked at it. It means a long turn before he can have another go. There'll be hell to pay for this.

Excuse me, said Cadbury, and she ran for the Ladies.

There were three cubicles in the room. Two were occupied and the middle one was vacant. The pressure in Cadbury's bowels began to increase intolerably as she half ran towards the open door. She began to drag her skirt up to her waist as she flung herself into the cubicle, slammed the door to, and ran in the bolt. She ground her bottom onto the cold porcelain without bothering to put the seat down. Wriggling her panties down to her knees, she splayed her thighs and kicked off her shoes in an ecstasy of release as she felt the huge churning movement of the excrement begin in her body. Knowing there was no longer any need to hold it back, she allowed herself the luxury of trying to fight it off. She enjoyed the delicious sensation of being over-powered and obscenely emptied by the uncontrollable need within her body. Her eyes closed, and her lips opened. She sighed with pleasure. In a climax of release, her evacuated wastes discharged and ran in the bowl.

Afterwards she lifted her body from the pan, stood up, and smoothed the skirt down over her legs.

With a shake of her yellow hair, she tugged at the steel chain and listened with contentment as the water flushed and churned the remains of her evacuation into the complex pipes and tunnels of the hotel's disposal system. She turned to the door and undid the catch. A slight noise caught her attention. She looked up. From the cubicles on either side, the grinning faces of two male Japanese looked down at her.

Outside, a church clock began to chime. In a long silence, Cadbury counted twelve. It was the hour of the horse.

10

It was a warm day in London, and Valerian enjoyed the walk to St. Christopher's Place. There were clouds in the sky, and he had taken his umbrella on his usual Capricornian principle of caution. He swung it now as he walked, to all intents and purposes a senior civil servant on his way to a business lunch with a colleague.

At the restaurant they led him up the short flight of stairs and towards the broad black table behind the screen where Incontro was already waiting.

Hello, John, said Valerian. I'm sorry I'm late.

He eased himself between the tables and sat down with his back to the wall. The man who was facing him knew the score. When you ate in a restaurant with Valerian, you arrived first, and you took a seat that left you vulnerable, and therefore likely to be honest. Valerian himself had a horror of being surprised, and he would only eat if he could be sure of sitting with his back to a wall, and preferably, as now, to a corner. He was fond of quoting a passage from *Across the River and into the Trees* in support of this preference. It didn't support it, but it added glamour. And Valerian, who had been graded four through a form of heart trouble, and hence missed all forms of military service in the grim days of conscription, had a quite unhealthy respect for the ways and foibles of such archaic hero projections as Hemingway's Colonel Cantwell.

He probably plays with a box of toy soldiers every night before he goes to bed was how Loyola had once put it as he petulantly peeled an apple on a file marked "Top Secret."

You know he doesn't, said Angeline, his male secretary. You know exactly what he does before he goes to bed.

It was true. The closed-circuit cameras were unloaded and perfunctorily played back once a month, and there were few aspects of Valerian's nightly rituals, from masturbation to cleaning his teeth, that had not been inspected and vetted *ad nauseam*.

The point is, said Loyola as he cut the pips away, that he *would* be playing with a box of toy soldiers if he didn't know about the cameras.

This was also true, or partly so. Valerian was a great lover of toys, both military and animal, and he had spent a good deal of time equipping himself a play alcove into which the eagle eyes of the cameras had so far failed to penetrate.

I was not born under the careful sign of the goat for nothing, said Valerian.

The Service would not have liked his Teddy bears and

his soft owls, and Magneto would never have let him hear the end of it.

While he settled himself in the corner and folded the black napkin over his knee, he smiled at the man on the other side of the table. He had known John Incontro before he worked for Sotheby's, and he enjoyed his old-fashioned English precision. He liked the stiff white collar and the small tight knot in his club tie. The three-piece tweed suit, with the soft chalk pin stripe and the knife-edge crease tucked out of sight below the table. It all gave an air of reliability.

But today the bread at Incontro's left hand was crumbled into a pile of bits. His hair was slightly disarranged. He seemed to have been sweating. The smile began to disappear from Valerian's face.

It went badly, he said.

Let's order first, said Incontro, recovering the initiative. I'm in no mood to be bullied, Valerian.

They inspected the huge brown folders offered to them by the Japanese girl with a gloomy detachment. Valerian knew exactly what he wanted. There was very little foreign food he could tolerate, and he had reduced the possibilities in this particular restaurant to a basic two on a previous visit. It took Incontro longer, but he was a professional.

Pilaff, with daikon and *shiitake,* he said at last.

Will you have a little *an* sauce, said the waitress.

Valerian played with his chopsticks. They were plain wood, and disposable. He had a strong fancy to bring a pair of special lacquered ones on his next visit.

What I had before, he said.

So what happened, said Valerian as he lifted a chunk of meat from his thin soup.

Incontro paused to pour himself another minute cup of saké.

The usual dealers were there in force, he said. It was the strongest sale we've had in several years. And the catalogue was pretty widely distributed.

Abroad as well as here?

Indeed. So I wasn't entirely surprised to see so many unfamiliar faces. On the contrary.

What did surprise you, asked Valerian.

Incontro swallowed a mouthful of saké.

The price for the first lot, he said. It was a good *katana*, unsigned, slim *koshi zori, shinogi tsukuri* . . .

Cut the cackle, said Valerian.

All right. But give me time. And worth about seven hundred pounds. Give or take a hundred. I knew that Tomayo wanted it, and so it was possible it would go a bit higher. He was there at the back with his girl. I kept my eye on him when the bidding started. It went fast up to five hundred with a couple of collectors slugging it out together. But I could see they had no chance. Tomayo came in at six fifty and he killed the first collector at eight hundred. The other came back and stuck it out to a thousand and ten. Tomayo bid a thousand and twenty, and the collector shook his head. I had the hammer up, and I was sure it was Tomayo's.

Incontro remembered the scene. It was always much the same. In the basement gallery about forty dealers and collectors were seated or standing, chatting or studying their green catalogues. A few had wives or mistresses with them, but most were alone. There was always a hunting air about an auction room. Incontro liked the expectant masculine tension and suppressed violence of the atmosphere. When he had come in up to his wooden box promptly at eleven o'clock, there had been a quick mutter of anticipation, and then a sudden hush. It was like a sports stadium or a gambling club.

He always paused before he started, to savor the feeling of the day. Below him the attendants in their gray coats waited beside the wooden racks of swords and the glass cases containing the furniture, the numbered groups of *tsuba, kozuka,* and *menuki.* One of them was already looking up with the first lot of the day carefully lifted in his hands, ready to walk forward and display it to the potential buyers.

Lot 1. *Katana.* Hundred pounds for it, he had begun that morning.

And the porter had walked around and held up the long blade in its *roiro* scabbard scattered with *aogai,* the greeny mother-of-pearl gleaming slightly on the polished back of the lacquer. As he saw it from above, it was like an offering, a sacrifice to placate the gods of fair play. The white faces of the bidders looked up in their ranks behind it, rather more than usual, nearly fifty perhaps, and several he didn't know.

When the bidding began, he had felt the usual urge of excitement, the sense of controlling and feeding the bids, of squeezing or teasing to suit his own prearranged plan of how the sale should go. It was like painting a picture in some ways, allowing a steady recession here, placing an odd feature there to catch the eye, distributing color and shape to form a coherent and satisfying pattern. Normally, that is, he thought to himself. But not today. He began to sweat more as he remembered.

I had the hammer up, he continued, watching the waitress begin to serve his pilaff, fragrant with the genuine savor of camellia oil. I never think it's the same with sesame seed, he inserted as he tucked the first mouthful neatly between his lips. Is your fish all right?

The suspense is killing me, said Valerian. You've missed your vocation. You should have been a thriller writer.

I thought that life was always a thriller for you boys, said Incontro.

It was true, Valerian thought while he examined with detached pleasure the serrated side of his salmon. He agreed with the Japanese that the look of a fish was at least as important as the flavor. Incontro was really a Chinese eater. He saw it all as sauces and odors, a meal for a blind man. But it was true, he reflected as he began to eat, returning to the thought he had digressed from. The Service attracted the type of personality that existed in a world of dreams. For Valerian, reality had no meaning. Whatever happened, happened as part of the novel or film unreeling in his fantasy, in which he had always a threatened role to fulfill against the determined but ultimately defeatable energies of an alien world.

For a moment he felt a chill of doubt. It was also true, he knew, of his attitude towards sex. For Cadbury, the world was a rich larder of immediate sensation, in which the avarice of her desires could be instantly titillated and satisfied. She knew this, and could exploit it more efficiently than any woman he had ever known. Which was why she possessed her unique position in the hierarchy of the Service. At the bottom, with everybody on top of me, as she had once put it.

You like being used, said Valerian.

I use by being used, she replied.

For Valerian, the world of sex was a complex ladder of rises and falls, of intrigues and relationships in which his insatiable need for controlled mystery and danger could be brought to a point of climax. It was always the moment before and the moment after he savored most. For him, the present was an avoidable pitfall. But it sometimes yawned before him, and its muscles gaped to engulf his philosophies. He had learned a lot from Cadbury, and he felt himself changing.

Incontro coughed.

I had the hammer up, he began again. I saw Tomayo's girl poise her pencil to write the price they had got it for in her catalogue, and I was about to bring the hammer down when I heard a voice from somewhere in the front row say:

Thirteen hundred.

He was Japanese, about fifty, with spectacles and a plain unobtrusive blue suit. I hadn't noticed him before. He looked a bit like a businessman looking for a souvenir on a day off.

You're going to pay for it, I thought. Tomayo was annoyed. I saw his lips tighten when he nodded for fourteen hundred. The man in the blue suit lifted his catalogue. Tomayo jerked his head. You could feel the tension rising. At that stage the price was double what the sword was worth, and it was the first item in the sale. The rest would undoubtedly go through the roof if this went on.

You were pretty excited, said Valerian as he laid a bone of his fish aside.

I was puzzled, Incontro replied. Here was a complete stranger bidding very high against the most famous dealer in the business for a fairly ordinary blade in a sale containing over a hundred. I tried to visualize the mounts again. The *tsuba* was signed, but not by anyone good.

What was the subject, Valerian asked.

It gave no help. Shiba Onko rescuing his friend from the water jar. Not very frequent, and not very interesting.

And the technique?

Very ordinary. The metal was *shibuichi, mokko* form decorated in *kebori,* copper and gold *hon-zogan.*

Valerian groaned.

So what happened next, he said.

The price was at sixteen hundred. The man in the blue suit to bid. So I thought I would push it a bit. When he lifted his catalogue, I looked straight in his eyes and said eighteen hundred. He never gave any sign he noticed. Tomayo had already bid two thousand.

Two thousand two hundred, the man said.

Tomayo bit his lip.

Two thousand five hundred, he said.

Three thousand, the man said.

There was a tense silence. Tomayo looked furious, and then suddenly relaxed, and cruel. He shook his head. I could feel the breath released from the whole room before the excited murmur began.

Sold for three thousand pounds, I heard myself saying.

And my assistant went around with his card to get the unknown buyer's name as we moved on to Lot 2.

Lot 2 was a *wakizashi*, a medium-sized sword with a nice *hamon*. *Gonome midare* of *nie* and *nioi*.

He remembered the flecks of cloud along the wave line of the tempering, that endless fascination of moving light.

And the same thing happened again, said Valerian, pouring himself a fourth cup of the saké.

Not quite, said Incontro. A different buyer. But again a man unknown to me. A Japanese of about thirty, very good-looking, with a sports jacket and long hair. He bid against Lucas for it, a Bond Street dealer. The price went up and up again, and he got it for twice what I'd have expected. The next six swords were all bought by Japanese I didn't know, one by the man in the blue suit again and the other five by separate individuals. The prices were all high.

I'm beginning to get the picture, said Valerian. Let me ask you two questions. First: was any sword in the sale bought by a dealer or collector who was not Japanese?

No, said Incontro.

He was irritated by Valerian in this mood. He would have preferred to retell the story of the sale at his own speed, with a blow-by-blow account of each bid and sale. . . . But, after all, he reflected, the man was paying for his lunch. And in a restaurant of his own choice.

Second, said Valerian: was any sword bought by a dealer or collector you already knew?

No, said Incontro, tugging gently at his tie.

And how many of these new buyers were involved, said Valerian as he sipped the last of his wine.

Incontro savored his moment, although he guessed that Valerian had already worked out the implications.

There were seven of them, he said. Seven samurai, re-acquiring a total of one hundred and eleven ancestral blades. All with different names. All writing checks on the same bank. All with rooms at the Savoy.

It's happened before, of course, he added, wiping his lips with his napkin. There was a sale in New York last year where the price of prints went through the roof. And it's well enough known that the big industrialists are acquiring the French Impressionists just as fast as they can lay hands on them. But swords have so far been a rising but predictable market. It's most unusual to find a new group coming into the field like this out of nowhere.

But it's not illegal, said Valerian.

Not at all, said Incontro. The only question is whether the market can possibly stand such a sudden and unforeseen inflation. I don't think it can. There's a clever old lad in Mitsubishi or somewhere who's going to get his financial fingers rather badly burned.

I wonder, said Valerian as he pushed his chair back.

In the street outside, a Japanese was photographing a small boy bouncing a ball in a doorway. He took meticulous care in aligning the camera to his eye, and he smiled with direct charm at the boy when he snapped the lens.

A hundred million of them, Valerian thought.

They're a fiendish lot, he said as he swung his umbrella.

A miracle that we won the war, Incontro replied.

I'm grateful to you, John, said Valerian. I'll be seeing you at the club.

He glanced at his watch as he walked away from Incontro up Wigmore Street. It was nearly two. They had eaten fast, and he would have time to walk the whole way back. It would help to focus his mind on the problem.

THE HOUR OF THE GOAT
2:00 P.M.

11

Cadbury first of all became aware of a curious rising and falling motion. In the strange speckled darkness inside her head, like the abstract chaos before the creation of the world, there was gradually this uneven kinetic sensation of rocking. In the morning, before waking, she was often aware of the blurred littoral between sleep and alertness as a sort of no man's land, a nightmare invasion beach where the creatures of night and horror were caught half-unawares for a moment before they had time to crawl back into the sea of dreams.

Today her arm seemed reluctant to move, and there was the kind of throbbing in her brain she associated with the aftermath of drunkenness, or the opiates. There was a thick feeling in her mouth, and a taste of something she could only partly identify as alcohol. But the strange rising and falling seemed to be outside the hazy confines of her body. A stab of sickness cut through the muzziness, and she urged her head to one side when a heave of retching began to strain at the muscles of her stomach. As her neck twisted, without, it seemed, moving very far from the horizontal plane she was lying in, a stream of vomit poured involuntarily from her mouth, and she opened her eyes to a metal bowl dashed with the blotchy excrement of her self-evacuation.

My Christ, said Cadbury.

Her eyes flicked upwards as her neck twisted back, and she stared at the curved metal shape of what seemed to be another huge bowl inverted above her. The muscles tensed in her arms and legs, and she made a convulsive movement to sit upright from the supine position she was fixed in. It was a second after nothing had happened that she realized something was holding both her wrists and her ankles in place. There was a sense of tight constriction in them, as if she were bound or nailed to a rigid framework. Once again, with a fierce, sudden concentration of energy, she forced her whole will into breaking loose from her fixed position and sitting up.

When nothing happened, and the force ebbed away from her extremities, a second stab of sickness came, and she twisted her neck to vomit again into the bowl apparently laid on a small high support beside her. She was aware of the dry sour taste of her intestinal fluids in her mouth, and again of the rocking movement outside her body, as if she were fixed in a swing or a roundabout. She began to run her consciousness over the parts of her body, ignoring the general impression and systematically testing the individual limbs and muscles. Everything seemed to be all right. She felt sore at the wrists and ankles, and she couldn't move, but nothing seemed broken or bruised.

Suddenly, she shivered. The most obvious fact about her position had failed to strike her. She was naked.

Cadbury began to digest the implications of her situation.

A slow prickling goose flesh ran up her legs, across her belly, and around under her buttocks and up her back. She felt suddenly exposed and degraded, laid out like a fish or a corpse for inspection or dismemberment.

As far as she could make out, she was lashed in a spread-eagled position to four supports at her feet and behind her head. Her legs were extended and arched downwards across the edge of a sort of rod or bar, perhaps even the rim of an ordinary table. Her arms were pulled back and arched down behind her out of sight and fixed or tied to a pair of supports. The middle of her body was arched up and held higher than her head on some kind of cushion or soft platform. She could feel a sort of moquette or velvet against the undersides of her thighs and buttocks.

Male sexuality at its most perverse, thought Cadbury.

She remembered a photographic session in Greek Street when the Service had sent her to do some checks on a suspect Italian politician. He had offered her a seat in what looked at first like a comfortable armchair, a good deal safer than the luxurious sofa that was the only alternative. She recalled how she had crossed her legs to allow him the sound of her sleek new silken tights. He had turned to pour out some drinks, there had been a soft hiss, and the chair had tipped up and back like a dentist's chair, with one difference. A long bar had come up between her calves, run forward to part her thighs and push up her skirt, and then slid away under her crutch out of sight. A pair of clamps had snapped shut around her ankles, and a sort of rounded cushion had thrust her belly upwards and away from her.

It was invented by Casanova, the Italian had explained

as he unbuttoned his trousers. You see I can spin the chair on its axis and enjoy you in comfort standing up. It is good for an old man like me with a bad back.

The pictures had been even better than Valerian had expected.

As her mind ran over this recollection, the element of fear began to drain away from Cadbury. She was used to accepting things as they were. It was one of her regular techniques to reduce the surprise and shock of the unfamiliar with a moment's reminiscence about some overcome disaster or shock in the past, and its effects were usually fast and helpful. It was unlikely, she told herself, that she was in for anything more horrific and painful than a sort of Japanese gang bang. Men were astonishingly easy to predict. It would have been a good deal more frightening if they had left her fully clothed. Her strongest armor was her own bare skin. Few men, of whatever propensities, had ever been able to resist the pull of that for long. She relaxed her muscles and began to breathe very steadily, with her eyes fixed in a semiunfocused way towards a point in the ceiling.

We have no time for your meditations, said a voice above her. You Western children are all so superficial. It took me nineteen years to understand the first thing about a blade of grass.

We must have a game of Go sometime, said Cadbury.

The man who had spoken was looking down at her through a pair of old-fashioned steel spectacles of the type familiar from wartime photographs of General Tojo. His face was long and bony, and he looked to be an extremely fit seventy-five. He was dressed in a silver kimono marked with the same leaves of the wild ginger plant as Yamaka had worn.

Tokugawa Yoshimitsu, he said, with a slight bow. I am a master of the second rank, and it would be a waste of your time. You could perhaps learn from my son. He is five.

Cadbury felt the sickness rising in her gorge again as the old man looked down at her, and she concentrated hard to contain and restrict its flow. It was no good. She vomited again into the bowl.

Clever, she said as she kept her eyes turned away from the old man. But I could do the same if I had you strapped down here after an overdose of morphine.

So why do you do it, the old man said. You are a woman devoted to the most skillful and extravagant practices of sexual endeavor. And you prostitute your talents in the service of a corrupt government. In Japan we should find you a noble and worthy employment as a geisha. In the eighteenth century, in the Yoshiwara, you would have entertained the most eminent samurai of the day. Perhaps only the daimyo, or even the shogun himself, would have courted your favors.

Or the managing director. Or the chairman of the board. With a prick like a flaccid eel, said Cadbury.

Yoshimitsu laughed. A delicate even shaking ran through his old body, and he reached down to his obi. Hanging from it on a silk cord was a small oblong box, suspended by a sort of toggle at his waist. He fingered the box, sliding the top compartment open and extracting something. It was a pinch of white powder, which he inhaled into his nose.

Cocaine, he said. You knew when Yamaka was screwing

you. Is it still screwing you call it? The words change so quickly.

I call it buggering, said Cadbury.

Yoshimitsu laughed again.

We could carry it more easily in an *inro,* of course, he said as he tapped the small box. But they usually ask to have one of the cases opened. With swords, it is easier. You declare the sword, and who is suspicious. It costs so much in itself. I think of it as the layer principle. If a man is convicted of theft, few think he is covering up for murder.

So your whole squalid operation is pinching antique swords as a way of smuggling snow out of England and into Japan.

What a curious idea, said Yoshimitsu, and the same delicate shaking laughter ran through his body again. What a very curious idea. We carry the cocaine for our own stimulus, not for the corruption of an already decadent society. If I had wanted to import this drug to Japan, I should scarcely have bothered with such a devious route through Gibraltar. And my business interests have long ago removed from me all need to amass further material wealth. I am a very rich man. I can afford to fill my nose and my mouth with whatever substances I require.

So what's on the menu now, said Cadbury.

Yoshimitsu had settled himself on a high stool at her right shoulder. He drew his kimono round him, and began to talk.

In a moment, he said. Let me tell you first of all where you are.

In a submarine, said Cadbury. I remember seeing it making

ready to go to sea this morning. This spacious little metal coffin couldn't really be in anything bigger.

The U-99 said Yoshimitsu. Under the command of Obersturmführer Schepke, it sank over ninety thousand tons of your English shipping between 1942 and 1945. It was sold as scrap to a Scottish dealer, who ended up keeping it in Loch Long as a souvenir. When he died, his son was more interested in the money than the associations. He advertised, and I bought it.

What happened to your own Imperial submarines, asked Cadbury.

They are all on the bed of the sea, said Yoshimitsu. The Emperor may have told us all to lay down our arms, but he never told us to hand the Yankees all our technology on a platter.

So you bought a German boat as the next-best thing.

I bought what I could get, said Yoshimitsu simply. I wanted a machine that would travel legally below the sea. It is not too easy. This ancient Nazi warhorse is a classified antique, and the world regards poor Yoshimitsu as a crazy old retired maker of motorcycles who likes playing with his war toys.

Instead of a sword smuggler.

I am not a sword smuggler, said Yoshimitsu patiently. Or not in the sense that you think. The only swords I have smuggled out of England and into Gibraltar are those we were unable to buy.

He glanced down at the gold watch incongruously strapped on his wrist under the silver sleeve of the kimono.

It is now the hour of the goat, he said. In London seven of my samurai have bought a hundred swords in your auction rooms at Sotheby's. In one hour they will empty your greatest museum at Bethnal Green. By tomorrow morning, when we put in at the harbor we are bound for in Wales, we shall have recovered the best of the swords in England.

A strange sweetness came into the old man's face, and he looked down reflectively at Cadbury.

I have a daughter in Wales, he said. The fruit of my love for an English girl I met long ago on a business journey. She has no idea she carries my blood, but I send her presents, like a rich uncle. It happens to be her birthday, and I have a kimono for her.

He looked down at Cadbury with a fatherly softness, and she remembered suddenly where she had seen that look before. It was Loyola, in the taxi home after their first night out, who had also seemed to assume this oddly paternal softness towards her.

She flexed her stomach muscles as she lay exposed, setting firmly aside the ways her thoughts were leading, back towards that strange incident with her own father that she tried so hard never to remember. She knew that she must fix her mind on the present, on the vital information that the old samurai was prepared, in his new mood, to reveal for her.

For a sword collector, she said, you seem prepared to go to unusual lengths to satisfy your hobby. I should have thought there were enough blades to keep you happy in Japan.

The old man's face darkened.

There are more swords in America than in the land they were made in, he said. In England, there are thousands brutally looted by your troops in the Burma campaign. These weapons are the symbols for us of the glory that departed with the Imperial rescript. On the basis of which we laid down our arms. I do not recognize that we ever surrendered. The war against the folly and decadence of the West is still on. It will always be. But it has to end by withdrawal, not by victory. We must re-establish a Japan untainted by commercialism and vulgarity, the Japan that existed before the Americans arrived. The return of our swords, by whatever means may be necessary, is as vital a preliminary to that as the founding of the kibbutzim in Palestine.

He smiled.

It is fitting, he went on, that a handful of the best of these swords from Britain should enjoy their last climax on the bloody sand where your own Lawrence fought for the freedom of Arabia.

In Israel, said Cadbury.

A cold, faraway look had come into Yoshimitsu's eyes. He began to talk more rapidly and intensely, as if to himself, ignoring the naked girl spread out before him.

In a few hours time our treacherous Prime Minister will arrive at Lod Airport on a state visit. He will find a reception committee of his countrymen ready to greet him in the manner he deserves—with a ring of swords.

You mean to assassinate him, breathed Cadbury.

We mean to purge him, and through him the decadence of a money-grubbing society. It will be the signal for our compatriots in Tokyo and Kyoto to initiate their armed rising. Before the week is out, my country will have returned to the noble isolation of my great predecessor, Tokugawa Ieyasu.

Perhaps once again, he murmured as he fingered the beautiful precise figuring on the lacquer of the *inro*, we can return to the era of peace and independence that produced such art as this.

Perhaps you can, said Cadbury. But not by a ritual killing of a head of state with a sheaf of antique razor blades. And particularly not on the soil of a foreign nation. The Israelis will massacre you.

I wonder, said Yoshimitsu, with a mysterious smile. I wonder. I think that side of things may be taken care of. We have allies in high places.

For a moment there was silence. Cadbury noticed the remote steady humming sound of the motors as the submarine drove its way forward under the sea.

Tell me one final thing, she said. What happened to the poor bugger who slit his belly in the Rock Hotel?

He was full of shame, said Yoshimitsu seriously. There were two swords at the school, and he took the wrong one. It was a grave offense to his pride, but he has absolved the shame. His honor is satisfied.

So the real sword was nicked by Yamaka, said Cadbury. And later used to kill him. Which is when the Service began to get interested.

The Service, said Yoshimitsu. Yes, he went on, reaching under his kimono, we have a lesson to teach the Service. Interference is trivial, but the use of a woman against us is humiliating. It must be punished. And in an appropriate way.

He paused, and clapped his hands. A door seemed to open in a bulkhead out of Cadbury's line of vision, and she suddenly saw a group of Japanese heads begin to gather and form a circle around her. The cabin was quite small, and it seemed to fill and crowd as more and more men came in and took up their positions. All seemed to be wearing traditional Japanese dress, marked with the three leaves of the wild ginger plant. The ship forged on, and there was a quiet rustling and shuffling, then stillness.

Yamaka, said the old man.

Cadbury saw the faces part, and one bent forward over her. The man she already knew so well was standing between her open legs, and she could feel the cool silk of his kimono brushing her thighs. While she looked up at him, he threw off the garment and let it slither over her body to the floor. He was naked to the waist, shining with some kind of oil, and the hard male muscles stood out and rippled as he flexed himself.

The instrument, said the old man.

Yamaka reached into the obi at his waist and lifted something in his hands. It was about seven inches long, smooth and black, with a fluted section topped by a rounded end. Yamaka caressed it in his fingers, ringed by the circle of impassive male faces.

This is a vibrator, said the old man. It is a new model, developed by Tokugawa Electrics, which is one of my subsidiaries. It is not yet on the commercial market, and we are anxious to do some final tests on it. As you know, the average vibrator is a limited stimulant. It will bring a woman to orgasm with only seventy-per-cent security of success. And substantially less in the case of a girl with a puritanical disposition. This new vibrator is more effective. We anticipate a success of one hundred per cent, and an escalation of desire for it. It has been estimated clinically that the average experienced woman can enjoy a series of about fifty connected climaxes. After that, the effect is more dangerous than pleasurable. In the case of rats, there have been some interesting results. With our new vibrator we anticipate an approximate synthesis of desire and orgasm, or shall I say of frustration and fulfillment, after something like ninety-five minutes. In other words, in about one hour and a half, my dear Cadbury, we shall have reduced you to an electric addict, screaming and satisfied in a series of two-second alternations, while you literally die of pleasure.

What if the battery goes, said Cadbury, watching the supple fingers of Yamaka play on the black plastic.

That is where the Russian-roulette element enters, said the old man with a vicious smile. It is possible that you will beat the machine. In which case we shall try again tomorrow with a stronger battery. When your body has been a little restored by human contact. Yamaka.

Yamaka flicked a switch in the vibrator, and a high whine began. He braced his legs against the inside of Cadbury's thighs and lowered the machine to her shoulder. When it touched the skin, a delicious rippling sensation tickled and massaged her. She allowed herself to relax under it as the Japanese ran the machine gently down around the platform of her rib cage, skirting the domes of her breasts and the broad even plain of her belly centering on the navel.

I like it, said Cadbury.

She tensed herself, resisting the sensuous flooding sensation from the skillful inquiring head of the little black machine as it eased its way down over her hips and along the outsides of her thighs.

He knows how to do it, she thought. He was starting her easy, breaking down her resistance with a gentle start. She remembered the touch of his fingers in the hotel bedroom at Gibraltar, and her body began to quiver with an uncontrolled spasm. As if sensing this, the machine nosed over her thigh and towards the exposed hairs around her groin. She quivered again, uncontrollably, and the machine seemed to press upwards of its own accord, trembling and shivering with its own contained joy. She could feel the moistness coming in her vulva, clenched her fingers, and let herself go. The only hope was relaxation, sticking it out. The first wave of intense pleasure began to shake her whole body when Yamaka nosed the machine over the lips of her vagina.

12

It had started to rain. The man from Securicor watched the big drops gather on the edge of the window frame and slither down over the shops and passing cars of Bethnal Green. He didn't like museum duty. There were no dogs, for instance. No helmets and long truncheons to swing. After a rather unfortunate incident at the Victoria and Albert, there had been a directive about the men trying to look as commonplace and unobtrusive as possible. Violence was not expected. The important thing was to keep a general eye on the well-being of the artwork. It paid just as well as running hard cash to banks in closed vans. And surely the men would enjoy a spell of just putting their feet up?

Bennett watched the rain grow heavier. It hissed and jumped from the gravel on the narrow arc up to the museum door. A few cars were parked on the verge, and their windows ran with water. Across the road an old woman bustled out of a grocer's with a newspaper held in one hand over her head. He looked at his watch. It was nearly three. The party of Japanese tourists was due any minute. He stared morosely at the circulating visitors amid the exhibition of Toulouse-Lautrec drawings on the ground floor. They looked wet and depressed, as if they had only come in to shelter from the rain.

Bennett pushed his chair back on the tiled floor with a slight screech. He had better be ready. He stood up, buttoned his jacket to the neck, and tucked his hands together behind his back. He began to saunter across the entrance hall. Twenty-three steps to the bookstall. Twenty-three steps back to where he had started from beside the cash window. After three weeks of the job he had acquired all the casualness and bored incomprehension of the professional museum attendant. He had even stopped bothering to ogle the oily-haired temporary girl with the postcards. For the first week he had put in his time chatting to her with a view to a possible lunch hour in one of the locked wings.

Get stuffed, she had said, more than once, when the conversation had grown explicit.

Such language, dear, he had replied.

The second week he had contented himself with a series of imaginative fantasies, in the course of which he had systematically exhausted her sexual possibilities. He was a man of small inventiveness, and her oily hair, he had decided, was the wrong smell. He didn't even bother to look now as she bent down for a pamphlet from a stack at the back of the stall.

Bennett glanced again at his watch as a further influx of soaking visitors pushed through the wooden doors. The Japanese were late.

In his office on the first floor overlooking the insipid beds of flowers in his forecourt, the museum Director stood at his long window and reflected on how things had changed. The last time he had had a special party to examine the sword collection, they had come from America. All tan faces and crew cuts. Going on about Iwo Jima and the landings in Guam.

You know, sir, I have fourteen of those little babies. Fourteen, one had said, when he had been allowed to handle one of the three Muromasas.

The Director had been past shuddering. They had dropped a Sadamune copy, breathed on a possible Masamune *tanto*. The one with the fourteen babies had even slid his fingers along the blade of an early *ken*. The Director had vowed that he would never entertain a party of Americans again.

You needn't worry, his superior had said. The tide is turning. In ten years we shall have the Nips themselves.

And in a few minutes the first wave would be here, the Director reflected as he watched the rain. He remembered a straw hut in Burma in just such a rain. Nearly thirty years ago. And then, too, he had been waiting for a party of Japanese. He shivered.

It was either the vulgarity of the victors or the arrogance of the defeated, he thought. And Kahn says that by the end of the century they'll have caught up with the Americans. Economically, of course. And suppose they want a bomb or two to express their catching up. What then?

They're late, he thought suddenly as his eye caught the eighteenth-century lantern clock on his table. Not like the Japanese to be late.

The driver of the Zodiac compressed his lips. In front of his eyes, the wipers cut an even swathe in the falling sluice of rain. He could see the impassive faces of the two behind in the Scimitar. They seemed reduced to a lacquer worker's perfection in the oblong of the rear-view mirror. He eased himself in his belt. The light remained steadily fixed at red.

Two minutes past, said the man on his left, in Japanese.

Despite the rain he was wearing dark glasses and an open-necked shirt.

It doesn't matter, said one of the three men in the back. Nothing matters. It will all work out.

These English lights, said the driver. They can't mend anything. No wonder their tankers are no use any more.

Five past three, said the man in dark glasses.

It doesn't matter, said the same man in the back again. They will wait for us. And grow a little uneasy. The Japanese are not expected to be late. It will all help.

All five men eased themselves in their clothes. They flexed their wrists and ankles. The Western tweeds sat lightly on their slight, muscular bodies.

The man beside the driver in the Scimitar was busy with his thoughts. He had run over the details of the plan several times and there was nothing that could go wrong. He had folded the back seats of the GTE down already, and the lock on the rear door was oiled and unlocked. He reached behind him as they waited at the light and stroked the top of the long object like a tightly rolled mattress.

Don't worry, Saito, said the driver. It will hold them all easily. Not a blade shall come to harm.

I wish we were there, said the first man.

He was fat, and sweating. The car heater was off, but it seemed to make no difference. The driver had to reach out repeatedly and wipe mist from the inside of the windshield.

I could make a fortune with car ventilators in England, he said. These American de-misters are useless.

Let's hope it will do the one twenty-five they claim for it, said the fat man.

It did yesterday, said the driver. Near enough.

He let in the clutch as the light changed. They turned off to follow the dripping shape of the blue Zodiac into the road leading to Bethnal Green.

I wish we had time, said the polished man of his own age in the well-cut two-piece suit. I hear you have an excellent collection of *art nouveau* glass at your home.

The Director had liked him at once. They had arrived seven minutes late, full of apologies and good will. They had brought this little present for the Director's wife. Unworthy. But perhaps he would accept on her behalf. An eighteenth-century silk kimono from Edo, made, without doubt, for a great daimyo's lady. He had felt the stress in the silk, and been full of delight. She would love it.

That's really most awfully good of you. Perhaps . . . Have you time to come in and drink some sherry with us this evening?

It was a move in the game of politeness, and he knew they wouldn't. But the praise of his glass was unexpected. And effective.

Better than the collection here, he had replied. Though the museum does have a fair piece or two of Massier pottery.

If only there were time, said the Japanese, with regret.

He turned to his six colleagues, and all shook their heads with expressions of polite sadness.

You see, our company is very demanding, the Japanese continued. We have done some good business in London. Yes. But we must return tomorrow to Osaka. And there are conferences to be enjoyed this evening.

He spread his hands, at ease in the Director's best Empire chair. The others were sitting or standing with an air of subdued anxiety. The Director sensed their desire to be seeing swords.

Shall we go and look at the collection, he said.

What a pleasure, the Japanese replied.

He was already on his feet. For a moment the Director remembered the man who had first come through the door of the straw hut. The rain glistening on his face, and on the metal of his submachine gun. He rose to lead the way.

As they walked down past French snuffboxes, and Regency fashion dummies, the Director explained the scope and arrangement of his collection.

As you'll see, he said, we have them in a little wing of their own. With a good row of Kuniyoshi prints on the wall to give the visitors an idea of how the blades were used.

The fat man knew this. He had spent a whole day in the museum dressed as an elderly woman, and the details of its layout, running, and security were familiar and memorized. It was useful to have worked as a kabuki actor. Even if he had never been good enough to be a national cultural treasure.

We have about seventy-nine blades on show, the Director continued. And a good deal of furniture. A few blades fully mounted, and the main body shown by themselves. We keep them oiled, and on metal hooks in the glass cases. With the temperature, of course, very carefully controlled.

He paused as he reached the bottom of the steps. His pressure on the warning bell had worked very well, and the heavy, impassive figure of Bennett was standing there to meet them.

This is Mr. Bennett. Who helps us look after the swords, said the Director.

He was democratic, and believed in introducing his staff on all possible occasions. The Japanese had already gravely bowed to his frowsty secretary.

Mr. Bennett, said the Japanese in the blue suit.

His colleagues all bowed. The one in dark glasses had decided that Bennett was out of condition.

Knows some tricks, he thought to himself. And fast and brutal. But lazy from underwork. And he isn't expecting trouble.

The fat man looked at his watch.

It should be all right, he thought.

The rain beat on the metal roof of the museum.

Would you open the cases, please, Mr. Bennett, said the Director.

They had entered the little wing where the swords were displayed, and Bennett had locked the security gates behind them. Elsewhere in the museum the crowds were dazedly walking around the furniture and costumes, the toys and the prints. In the huge vaulted iron gallery there was a shuffling and cooing sound, as if a large number of doves were settling. The soft movements of human feet and voices continued while Bennett opened the first case.

Downstairs in the hall, the oily-haired girl was selling postcards. The attendant on duty at the cash window was taking money for tickets. In the Director's office, his ugly secretary was telephoning her boyfriend. The Assistant Director, who had the afternoon off, was at the cinema. The Japanese in the blue suit tensed himself as the first set of blades was laid bare. The moment was about to arrive.

He stepped forward and gently lifted a long, simple *katana* into the air, delicately balancing it by a pressure on the tang. His thumb rubbed the signature.

An unlucky blade, he said.

But a lovely one, said the Director.

It was the last thing he said for a long time.

The driver of the first car hit the Securicor man very expertly across the neck. He had stationed himself on Bennett's right, and the chop had a lot of force. There was never any chance he would recover or make a sound. The fat man caught and snapped the cord of the walkie-talkie before Bennett hit the ground.

If you make any noise, said the man with the dark glasses to the Director, I shall blind you. Very painfully. With my fingers. You served in Burma, and you have seen it done. And believe me I can do it.

He stood relaxed before the Director, one hand on his shoulder, the other with the first and second fingers extended into a savage, obscene prong a few inches from his eyes.

He means it literally, said the man in the blue suit, spinning the blade in his hand. Literally. No sound. No words. Nothing. Now one question. To which you will nod for yes or shake your head for no. I warn you. I may know the answer already, and be testing you. And if you lie, Saito will blind you. So don't. This is it. Are there any other guards in the building?

The director shook his head.

Very good, said the Japanese, and he dipped the sword as if for a signal. Four of the Japanese vaulted over the locked gate and moved swiftly away downstairs. The fat man lifted the key from Bennett's belt and began to unlock the cases of swords. The man with the dark glasses remained exactly where he was, his rigid fingers poised before the Director's terrified, furious, and desperate eyes.

In the long silence, the Japanese in the blue suit allowed himself to relax. He reflected on what was happening while he waited. Outside in the rain, two samurai had already opened the back of the GTE and were manhandling out the rolled wash-leather case in which they would wrap the blades. In the foyer, another had engaged the attention of the girl with the postcards, and was mingling praise for her loose body with desire for the more awkwardly placed pamphlets under her counter. She would see and care little about what was going on in the hall. At the ticket window, the fourth samurai was blocking the grille while he searched in his pockets for a pencil to write some message with. The patient old man in the box was waiting and attentive. The Japanese were always so polite. And they were rare visitors. The wet English public would take no interest, or assume it was all for television. And the rain would go on falling on the good and the evil as it always did, without discrimination and without interference.

As the last of the blades was fitted neatly into its place in the long, unrolled leather case, the Japanese in the blue suit allowed himself to smile.

Don't worry, he said to the Director. It wasn't your fault. You will die. But not today.

He nodded to the man in dark glasses, who hit the Director across the neck. He seemed to be trying to fall so as not to spoil the crease in his trousers.

Take the blades down, said the man in the blue suit.

He watched four of the samurai fold, roll, and lift the leather case. It looked very much like a mattress, inoffensive and natural. They humped it on their shoulders and eased it over the gate. Vaulting over, they lifted it again and began to walk easily down the stairs and through the exhibition to the main hall. As they walked through, the Japanese in the blue suit paused to smile at a little boy who was examining them curiously.

I'll bet that you could carry a Japanese bed like that all by yourself, he said.

He bowed to the child's mother, and extended a bag of sweets.

Quality Street, Mum, said the child as he took a handful.

I'm glad you like them, said the Japanese.

In the car, he sat beside the driver. This time the Zodiac followed, with the car radio on. In the Scimitar, the man in the blue suit leaned back in the reclining seat. He closed his eyes.

So easy, he said.   So easy.

The rain splashed from a puddle onto the sheen of the fiberglass as they cornered fast and merged into the rush-hour traffic.

Things move slowly on a wet day. No one was bothered that the Japanese wing of the museum was closed. The bodies of the Director and the Securicor man were out of sight from the stairs. It was well after four before the secretary decided to ask if the Director needed anything.

I remember now. The Japanese are always drinking tea, she thought.

She adjusted her skirt and bobbed primly down to the Japanese wing. It was locked, and no one was there. So she went down to the ticket window to ask if the man there knew where the visitors were.

They've gone, Miss Aldridge, the girl with the oily hair called out. About half an hour ago, I think. I thought you'd have known.

They never tell me anything, she thought as she walked back up the stairs.

THE HOUR OF THE MONKEY
4:00 P.M.

13

Loyola was feeling drowsy, as he always did about teatime. He sat in the heavy Chippendale chair at his leather-topped writing table and toyed with his Preiss figurine. It had cost him six hundred pounds at Sotheby's the previous week, and depicted a boy in very tight silky trousers leaning on a rather ambiguous tree. The feel of the ivory would normally have sent his mind rather quickly along one particular track, but today his thoughts were on other matters. Outside the long Adam windows, a sharp wind had started to blow the remaining leaves on the high elms in the park, and Loyola watched with a sleepy sense of disturbance as his mind grappled and slid away from the problem of the swords.

My God, he said suddenly, hearing the clock on his mantel begin to chime four.

He shook himself, and straightened his tie. It was already immaculate, but Loyola was a fastidious man. He pressed the switch of the intercom on his desk.

Angeline, he said, would you ask Valerian to come in a bit sooner? If he's free, of course.

And you'd like some tea, said the voice from the loud-speaker. With cream and sugar. And something to eat with it.

I'm hungry, Angeline. I'd like the whole thing, said Loyola. The whole thing.

Of course, darling. But later, said the voice.

Up yours, said Loyola, with characteristic vulgarity.

Valerian, he said a few moments later as the door opened without a knock, and Valerian entered. I might have been looking over my privates. I wish you'd knock.

Valerian knew better. It appealed to Loyola's perverse exhibitionism to be caught unawares by his subordinates.

I'm sorry my timing was out, said Valerian as he swung his leg over the arm of the easy chair in front of the desk. It must be frustrating for you. Had you meant to be having a shit in the wastepaper basket?

He looked across at the stocky, slightly bald man on the other side of the desk with a kind of defensive aggressiveness. He had worked for Loyola for nearly twelve years, and there was little about his business methods or skills that he didn't know. Loyola was a genius. He had the brightest mind, and the most degraded imagination, of anyone Valerian had ever met. The Service was his personal creation, and there were times when it struck Valerian as the most complex work of art since the death of Proust. He stopped his thoughts and frowned. Loyola could make you feel as if he had just invented you, and your role in his novel was going to be an exceptionally disgusting one.

I like the figure, he said.

I thought that Chiparus would be more your sort of thing. But yes. It is nice.

The door opened again and a young man came in carrying a loaded tray of tea things. He was wearing strawberry-red leather trousers, which creaked as he walked. Around his groin the skin seemed to have been polished with saddle soap.

Angeline, said Loyola. You make me lick my lips. How can I possibly keep my mind on my tea?

The young man pouted, and laid the tray on a circular mahogany table in the middle of the room. He made a substantial meal out of bending and rolling his buttocks while Loyola walked around the desk and came towards him.

Don't worry. I'll be mother, said Loyola, brushing the young man's waist with his hand.

Angeline lowered his body provocatively over the tray. His groin arched above the rounded peak of the silver muffin dish. He reached down with both hands and slowly lifted the lid off.

Would you like a bite, he said.

Excuse me, Valerian, said Loyola. You can watch, if you like.

Valerian rose to his feet and stood with his hands on his hips as Loyola ran his hand over the zipper of the boy's trousers.

Not a bite, he said. A handful.

Valerian walked across to the table and took the muffin lid from Angeline's hands. They were trembling slightly. He laid the lid aside and took a piece of hot buttered toast from the interior tray.

Awfully good, he said. You should have some.

And he pushed his right hand with the hot toast right into the boy's mouth, making him gag and choke. As he did so, Loyola shifted his hands, pulled the zipper right down, and had his left hand inside the boy's underpants, fingering and chafing at the firm, sprung arch of his bent penis, penned and checked like a bow in the nylon.

Valerian took another piece of toast and munched with pleasure. He carried the tray with him over to the window and stood with his back to the room while they gave each other what they wanted. He listened to the soft noises, the gasps and slithers as they felt and massaged each other.

Oh, now, please, Daddy, now, one voice said.

He can't watch, said the other roughly. He doesn't want to see his boss being buggered.

Oh, now, please. Oh, now.

When Valerian turned a little later, Loyola was leaning back on the front of the writing table. His trousers were undone at the waist, and he was panting. Angeline looked as immaculate as when he had come in.

See you later, he said to Valerian. Enjoy your tea.

Would you pass me some toast, Valerian, said Loyola, tucking his shirt in and lowering himself into an easy chair. I feel better for that.

I'm sorry, said Valerian. You can still surprise me.

That's why I run it still, said Loyola. Now give me the toast.

As he munched the butter-soaked bread with a loud, sucking sound, Loyola looked hard in Valerian's eyes.

Humiliation is power, he said. I taught Cadbury that. And you know it, too. But you still have your father fixation. Loyola has got to be God. And God is never seen with his pants down. Now listen, Valerian.

With a sudden agile swoop, he was out of his chair and

standing above Valerian. Cold-bloodedly, he reached down and grasped him roughly in the groin.

I could make you come, said Loyola. Against your will. And pretty quickly. Now tell me about the sale.

Stepping back, Valerian felt the horror and shock of those brutal hands deliberately massaging his private parts. He knew the rules, and had worked by them for years. He shivered, and swallowed.

Loyola frowned down at the Preiss figurine, cradled in his cupped hands. He had listened without comment as Valerian gave him a full account of all that Incontro had told him about the morning at Sotheby's. Now he sat silent, thinking.

You know what the situation is, he said after a time.

I think so, said Valerian.

About the politics, as well as the swords?

Yes.

How much does Cadbury know? said Loyola.

Valerian tapped his fingers on his knee. He had been wondering about this since lunchtime.

She could easily have learned it all in Gibraltar, he said. I mean, as well as finding out what we wanted her to. And making contact. She's pretty ingenious when she needs to be.

Loyola, said Loyola as the telephone rang.

Valerian watched his fingers tap swiftly over the scrambler switches.

Thank you for ringing, Masters. Quite a business for you.

Loyola began to whistle as he put the receiver down. It was a tuneless noise.

They've cleaned out Bethnal Green, he said. A total of seventy-nine swords. No casualties. But the security man and the Director have had a bit of a roughing up, it seems.

Let's eat the cake, said Valerian. It seems to be a choice between lemon-meringue pie and chocolate *gâteau*. Which do you prefer?

He paused inquiringly with knife in hand. Loyola eyed the cakes with a detached thoughtfulness.

There is another aspect of the matter, which you may not be aware of, he said. I'll try the lemon-meringue pie.

He munched in silence for a moment and then he began to talk. And Valerian listened while the rain beat on the window like the sound of tears.

14

The noise of the engines must have changed. When she awoke from her troubled sleep, she was aware of a different sensation in the multiple web of pressures and vibrations that formed the background to her consciousness. There was still the numbed throbbing in the middle of her body, the sense of a sort of twitching flicker in her head, as if a light were endlessly going on and off, and the dry sandy taste in her throat. But for a long time, hours, days perhaps, there had been another sensation, a deep background pulsing and rolling, unchanged however much the others altered.

Once, when she woke, Cadbury thought she must have died and been resurrected in a Japanese hell of vaginas, where the sinners damned for lust and fornication were receiving their punishment. Always above her head there had been the sweating curved metal of the bulkheads, the painted bolts of the fastenings, the occasional glimpse of some sliding movable, which had been stirred in a more than usually heavy swell in the submarine's movement. Sometimes Yamaka or the old man had come in to gaze impassively down at her as she lay and rested, her limbs flung out or curled together on the cheap sheets of the cabin bunk. On one occasion she had listened as in a dream to the steady murmur of their conversation in the smooth, beautiful choked flow of their language, like the blocks of ice melting in the walls of an igloo. She had drifted away, back into her fire and pain.

Twice more they had taken her out and carried her through to the other cabin, where she had been strapped and spread-eagled over the iron table. She remembered the serious impassive faces of the men when they had filed in, the smell of Yamaka's body as he had stepped between her parted legs, the grim nod of the old man's head as the operation had been resumed. She shuddered now, and her muscles convulsed, pulling her body together in a clenched knot.

The submarine must be moving more slowly. She was aware of an irregularity in the steady pitch and roll, a sense of some questing, more cautious progress beginning. She eased the tight ball of her limbs, and ran over the implications.

We're surfacing, she thought.

She remembered Yoshimitsu's reference to the auction at Sotheby's, and the planned theft at Bethnal Green. What was it he had said? Something about taking on board the swords at a harbor in Wales. Her mind dissolved for a moment into lightning flashes of disintegrated sensation. It was as if a heavy rock band kept suddenly starting to play full blast in front of her eardrums. She squirmed with a kind of stale exhilaration, a disgust for ecstasy. The vibrator had begun to work on her by a series of exhausted echoes, feeding back the initial impulses like a computer reshuffling its data inputs. She lapsed into half-sleep.

She was walking over an uneven red surface towards a huge bifurcated arch. Her feet kept stumbling on hidden bumps or sinking slightly in the soft substance of the ground itself. There was a hollow roaring noise in the distance, and a strong stench of something rotting. She stumbled again, and pitched forward onto her hands and knees. Her palms slid over something warm and moist. It gave a little when she pressed on it to rise. Again she moved forward towards the arch. Overhead there seemed to be a remote dark roof, as in a cathedral. She began to pant with exertion.

Suddenly, the hollow noise increased in volume, and she felt a throbbing in the red surface under her feet. As it grew in force, she was flung down and suddenly swept up in a cataract of icy fluid, thrown and swung forward towards the central pillar of the arch.

No, she gasped. Please, no.

She was aware of her hair spreading out on the fluid like weed, her limbs floating, her mouth opening and closing. The clothes on her body seemed to be dissolving and flowing away, leaving her cool and naked.

No more, she panted. No, no more.

She was aware of the arch above her head, its red lips dripping with a kind of salt or blood. The surge of the fluid flung her through and suddenly lashed on a wall of stiff white. The noise had been magnified to a high intense blare, vibrating and re-echoing in a tight smaller space. Her whole body seemed to be softer and wetter, more flexible and pliant in the drift of the currents within the surge. She felt her waist flex and grip.

Now, she heard herself gasp. Now, please.

Suddenly, she was dropping. As if weightless and disembodied, she was hurtling in a tube of crystal through a long tunnel of streaked red. It seemed to go on forever, without sense of falling or rising, up or down. Only the enormous speed within close dimensions.

Please never end, she gasped. Please never end.

She was melting into oil. Her belly seemed to have opened and poured out a thick precipitate, encasing her whole torso and lower body in a protective membrane. She felt enclosed in this as in a plastic envelope watching and feeling the hammer and rush of the fluid as in a dream within a dream.

When she woke, she was lying on a sort of muddy beach. As far as she could see, there were dim scattered fragments of material, organic and rotting. It smelled like a sewage plant. When she became aware that the fluid that had carried her here had receded, she tried to sit up and examine herself. She reached down to touch her groin, instinctive in her thought for her sex.

She screamed. Her hand was on a starfish. With clawing fingers she tore at it, struggling to pull it away from her belly. It came out with a plop of suckers.

She screamed again. Her hand was inside herself. She ran it up and over her chest, scrabbling to find the safe, reassuring femininity of her two breasts. Her nail scratched on a hard, smooth substance, ran forward, was on the carapace of a gripping crab. As she tore at it, it broke free, like the cup of a piece of armor. Her hand slithered on, desperate for the living woman flesh to be there underneath. The fingers dived, gripped. There was something there, soft and moving in her hand. It came away, red and dripping before her eyes.

She shuddered with terror and threw the thing on the ground. It lay oozing with red, still pulsing with a steady forceful movement. In fascinated horror, she watched until it heaved slowly to a final halt. With a hiss, it deflated, and sank into the mud.

Kneeling, she lifted her hands to her face. They were cold and horny, with tongues that licked her eyes.

Please let me wake, she whispered. I swear I'll never do it again.

But she knew as she felt the snakes coiling up her thighs that she would never wake. She was doomed to the dream of life until she died.

———

This time when she really woke, the noise of the engine was sharper, and clear. She could hear what sounded remotely like the wash of tides against the hull of a ship. There was a kind of bustle and expectancy in the far-off voices of the crew behind the bulkhead wall.

We must be coming in, she thought.

An excitement stabbed into her brain. She felt suddenly more in control of her flow of sensations. The submarine must be near to port. They would no doubt soon be in the harbor and ready to embark the cargo of swords. From what Yoshimitsu had said before the second operation, they intended to continue their experiments with the vibrator after they put to sea again. Therefore, they would not be intending to kill her or leave her in Wales. And they would be less on their guard while preoccupied with the embarkation. If there was to be a chance of escape or survival, it would have to be taken soon.

When Cadbury realized that she was still capable of consecutive thought, she felt a new surge of energy in her body. The irrational trembling and jerkiness seemed for the first time to be possibly under her control. She began to feel a faint sense of the concept of time. For an indefinite period, her brain had been a vessel of dreams and visions, an endless flux of horrific or pleasurable voyages over which she had had no control, and in which she had taken only a detached and intermittent interest. The schizophrenia of perception had separated her physical pain from her mental exhilaration or torment, and her total being had long ceased to suffer as consistently as the Japanese had supposed it would.

The vibrator had failed for a simple reason. On the first

occasion, Cadbury had endured a series of nearly fifty electrically induced orgasms of varying intensity. Her experienced body had absorbed and responded to these with a kind of delicious joy. But she had not finally died of pleasure. She had fainted with pleasure, sinking into a pit of exhausted and satisfied absence from which it had taken them several hours of speculation, massage, gentle beating up, and drugs to revive her. On the second occasion, she had realized, as they had not, that the vibrator could never win, unless she let it. Her body continued to respond and react to the electric impulses, but her mind was gradually disconnected from the pleasure of, and hence the desire for, the physical response. It became increasingly the vehicle for a succession of uncharted trips into the heights and depths of her unconscious mind. While her body writhed and twisted in the throes of its climaxes, her mind swept away and sailed into the remote wilderness of the harmonic present, sifting and prospecting of its own accord through the endless riches in the bottomless mine of now.

For anyone less familiar than Cadbury with the effects of acid, or the results of deep meditation, the consequence might well have been complete psychological breakdown. As it was, she allowed herself to accept and enjoy whatever happened. If it pleased her, she laughed. If it frightened her, she screamed. If her body wanted to convulse, it convulsed on its own. And so she survived in a double detachment. Physically unable to enjoy any further sexual excitement in her mind, and hence unable to set off the required mechanism of frustration and desire the Japanese needed to torture her to death. Psychologically free from the long-term effects of the complete disorientation of perception her mind was treating her to. It would take her a short time to recover her fitness, she realized, but only if she let the Japanese see what was really happening was she likely to be really hurt. The important thing was to prevent them from giving up the project in favor of something more directly and permanently brutal and maiming.

So Cadbury had been beaten up and drugged no more. The third operation had taken place like the second one, with the Japanese under the impression that she was rapidly reaching the end of her tether and that one or more final sessions would cause her to collapse and die. For this reason, as Cadbury now confirmed with a slow movement of her legs, they had omitted a sensible precaution. She was not tied up.

You bastards she thought. I'll beat you yet.

While Cadbury listened, she became aware that the engine noise was again changing. There was a sudden increase, a rapid vibration, the sound of voices, then silence. She strained her ears to the wash of waves. It seemed as if the submarine was at a standstill.

In the silence, Cadbury moved. She lifted her head, shook her hair, and looked around the cabin.

She was lying in the upper bunk of two in a cabin that contained four bunks in all, the other two being arranged one above the other a couple of feet away. There was no other furniture except a fixed table with a mirror above it in the bulkhead facing the iron outline of the closed door. She was alone.

Propping herself on her elbows, she flexed the muscles in her calves and thighs. Nothing seemed broken, or cramped.

She moved her right arm, eased up the sheets and slipped them off her body. She looked down its length, twitching a little, but supple and unmarked. She touched the tips of her nipples, felt them grow firm.

I really do seem to be all right, she thought.

Naked as she was, it was easy to check everything. And it all seemed to be in working order, at any rate as long as she lay flat.

O.K., she thought. Now for the big picture.

Compressing her lips, she lifted herself to a sitting position and swung her legs over the edge of the bunk. She dangled her legs, swinging them loosely, her hair falling over her face while she supported herself on her arms.

A wave of dizziness hit her. She fell back, rolled on her side, and vomited, taking care to do it as quietly as she could, stuffing her head under the sheet, and allowing the sticky liquid to splay over the flesh of her belly. The fit ended, and she lay gasping for breath. She remembered stories of people dying of their own swallowed vomit as she wiped her body clean on the undersheet.

They had fed her, she seemed to remember, at regular intervals. It was hard to recall quite when, or how. But she felt a sense of Yamaka's impassive face, and bowls of rice being lifted to her lips.

She raised her eyes from the sheet. On the wall of the cabin, a foot away from her eyes, a purple spider was crawling towards her. Its legs were covered with matted fur, and it moved with a slow somnambulistic inevitability. Behind it, a long gray web trailed and swirled over the foot of the bunk. It began to flow up over her knees as the spider approached.

Her muscles bunched with terror. The tendons in her calves went rigid. Before she could stop herself, she had screamed with fear.

When the cabin door was kicked open a few minutes later, Cadbury was again in the twilight interim between illusion and reality. She could feel the texture of the web on her skin, the sticky toils brushing her face as she fought to free herself, wrenching and straining on the vomit-stained sheets as the huge face of the spider came closer and closer to bite at her eyes. Half of her knew that she could drag her mind free of the terror if only she made a last superhuman effort. Half was aware of the necessity to remain in the grip of the terror, somehow to convince whoever came through the opening door that she was still under the spell of her madness.

She was aware of the spider speaking. Outside the web two men were hefting a sort of heavy mattress onto one of the other bunks. They seemed to be pleased with the spider's words. They laughed and pointed at her. One of them put his hand through the web and pushed her shoulder. They spoke together in Japanese, gesturing at her and at the other bunk.

Fuck the spider, screamed Cadbury. Please leave me alone.

The men laughed again. One of them reached in and stroked the spider behind its ear. It purred and nuzzled him. They both laughed when they went out, leaving the cabin door open. Cadbury could hear their feet receding, and then the clank of shoes on the metal of something. Their voices seemed to climb out of hearing.

Inside her twisting thoughts, the realization came that she had to make her effort now. With both hands she reached up and took the spider by the mandibles, crushing its bony furred body in her fingers. It became soft, ashy, and fell to pieces as she tore at the strings of the web. There was a hideous smell of burning tissue, and then she was free.

She sat up, clearheaded. The two Japanese had gone. The sound had been the clunk of their feet on the rungs of the metal ladder in the conning tower. They had brought something into the cabin and gone away for something else. Leaving the door open to get in again easily.

When Cadbury's feet hit the floor of the corridor, she felt a chill strike into her. An icy resolution froze and controlled her movements. Like a cat, she slid to the space below the ladder. The submarine seemed to be empty. Her eyes traversed the length of the curved metal to a closed door at the other end. A bank of dials confronted her beside the captain's desk. From the top of the conning tower, a breath of cool air came in, and the bright light of the outside world. She breathed deeply, sucking the strength of escape into her lungs.

She had no means of knowing how long it would be before the Japanese came back, or indeed whether the others were still below decks. If only two men were doing the work, while the others rested or walked to stretch their legs on firm ground, there was a chance she could gain a vital breathing space. She looked around for a weapon.

Suddenly, it came to her. There was only one thing to use. She turned and ran back to the cabin, reaching up and unfolding the heavy mattress the two men had hoisted in onto the bunk. Her finger ripped at the laces that held it bent over and closed. As they came loose, the material sprang back, and she caught it in time to spread it flat on the bed.

They lay there in neat sheaths of cloth around the wood of the scabbards, the seventy-nine swords from the museum in Bethnal Green. The hilts of the blades lay towards her hand, a choice for a prince or an executioner, the meticulous work of the craftsmen perfected in *menuki* and *fushi-kashira* around the terrible unpolished iron of the tangs. But there was no time to choose or think. Already she could hear the remote echo of the voices returning. Soon their footsteps would be on the metal of the ladder.

Valerian, she whispered, help me to choose right.

She slid the longest of the swords from its cloth holster, folded back the mattress, and ran to the space at the foot of the conning tower. There was nowhere to hide. Watching their boots as they clumped down the ladder, lumping something between them, she prayed they would be too preoccupied with its weight to look aside. She backed along the corridor away from her cabin, sliding the blade from its scabbard in her hand.

The metal of a door felt cold on her back, and a bolt pressed into her spine as she felt the sharp steel of the sword blade slide loose. The scabbard fell to the floor with a slight clatter, but the noise of the men's feet and voices was too loud for it to matter. One of them was standing looking up now, his arms raised and cradling one end of a long box. He backed towards her with it as the other man eased himself down. Holding her breath, she squeezed her naked body on the metal of the door, watching his rough tweed trousers edge closer and closer. The twine on the sword hilt scored her palm.

The other man appeared in the opening, looking over his shoulder away from Cadbury. If he turned to face his companion, he would be staring straight in her eyes. The first man began to walk forward again away from Cadbury, and the second man backed, still looking for safety over his shoulder. Together, they edged the long box through the corridor and towards the cabin.

As they walked, Cadbury eased herself off the door and forward. She lifted the sword in both hands, holding it out in front of her. She moved on tiptoe, naked as the spirit of vengeance, oblivious except to what she must do.

At the cabin door, the first man spoke, and paused. Then he lowered his end of the box to the floor and edged around the side to the man at the back. Together they lowered the back of the box and knelt side by side to push it along the floor into the cabin. For a moment their two heads were close together, low in the doorway, inclined over the end of the long box like the bearers with a coffin.

Cadbury put all her fear and hatred, all her muscular tension, all that she had learned in the Service and in meditation, into one long circular swing of the blade. Back it swept over her shoulder, round, and then down in a hard fast arc across their shoulders. The first man seemed to sense at the last moment that something was wrong. He was starting to turn as the edge cut him across the neck, sliced through, and left his head hanging forever on a half-realization of what had happened. The other man stayed in his first kneeling position, and the *kissaki* struck through his brain below the eyes.

Neither made any sound. And as the blood began to seep and flow from their necks across the coffin of swords, the naked woman they had tried to torture, and who had killed them, was on her way back into the freedom of the world.

The Hour of the Cock
6:00 p.m.

15

Cadbury paused at the top of the conning tower. With one hand, she leaned the sword against the metal rim, with the other she smoothed back the hair from her eyes. Very slowly, she lifted her face and looked over the edge, poising her body on the rungs below her.

Mercifully, it was dusk. Immediately below the submarine, which seemed to be moored at a sort of jetty, there was the upright mast and tackle of a small sailing ship. It looked beached, and unused. To the left of this, a long white-painted building with a round bow window could be seen. It might be a hotel, she thought. On the other side, there was the water of a small harbor, empty except for the submarine, and, far off across a bay, a line of distant hills. Beyond the hotel there seemed to be a path rising towards some sort of village or settlement. There was no sign of the other members of the crew. They were obviously either in the hotel, if that was what it was, or farther off up the hill.

Cadbury smoothed her mouth with her hand. She was lucky. She was free, she had a weapon, and there might even be the means to get something to cover herself with in the building. She realized that this would rapidly become a necessity as she shivered suddenly with cold. The exhilaration of escape and the rush of energy the killing had produced could last her only a little longer. It would be possible to try returning and stripping one of the corpses, but she had no taste for going back down the ladder towards the accusation in those severed heads.

Lifting herself carefully over the edge, she began to clamber slowly down the ladder on the outside of the conning tower. As her feet touched the wet deck, she slithered and clutched at the side of the metal for support. The sword slipped from her hand and fell away. She reached out to stop it sliding into the water, but it had hit the sea with a quiet splash and sank before she could get a hold.

Regaining her balance, she edged around the conning tower and looked quickly to right and left along the shore. There was a gangplank from the bow to the bank, and the water chopped below this with a low hiss in the rapidly gathering darkness. Steeling herself, Cadbury ran along the deck, stumbling and slithering in the wet. She crossed the plank, paused, and ran for the darkening wall of the hotel twenty yards away.

Panting against the whitewashed stone, she listened intently to hear if anyone seemed to have noticed her escape. There was no sound except the lap of the water, and the occasional sigh of the wind. She shuddered with the cold as she began to inspect the building for a way in. There seemed to be no lights, which suggested that it might be unoccupied, since it was now almost completely dark.

Very carefully, she inched her way along the wall towards what appeared to be the front door. As she reached the end of the wall, she could see that it was indeed a hotel, but that it seemed to be closed. There was a door, and what looked like a reception area behind it. Stepping forward, she pushed the door. It was locked.

Not surprisingly, said Cadbury.

Turning to look for another way in, she felt a sudden soft pressure against her calves. A twinge of horror shook her.

Christ, not again, she said.

As she looked down, the pressure flowed around and was succeeded by a slight nip in the flesh of her calf. She sighed with relief. It was a cat.

Bending down, she lifted the cat in the air. He mewed with pleasure, and she put a finger on her lips.

Shsh, boy, she whispered, putting him down. Will you show me how you get in?

The cat examined Cadbury in the dark. He seemed to approve, and pushed himself against her legs again to prove it. He was a small, very fluffy long-hair, and his eyes gleamed like searchlights. As if he understood her message, he began to run into the undergrowth to the right of the door, pausing to look expectantly over his shoulder.

Good boy, said Cadbury approvingly.

She followed lightly as the cat ran to a window on the ground floor. With a leap, he had settled himself on the sill, and stared thoughtfully at a small space at the top.

The wind howled as Cadbury glared at the window.

Anything for a laugh, she said, and hoisted herself onto the sill beside the cat. Reaching up, she found that her arm could work in and down to the catch. With a bit of fiddling, she was able to push it free, and the casement swung open with a creak.

The cat leapt in, and Cadbury followed.

Upstairs in the hotel, Cadbury felt her way in total darkness along what felt like a carpeted corridor. She had followed the cat into a long, curving room faintly lit by the light from the window. It had been full of tables covered, perhaps for the winter, with draped cloths. Beyond this, she had negotiated her way into a hall, a vague mist of dark shapes with a hint of a huge ornate baroque-style fireplace. Her hand had found the soft ridge of a sofa back, and she had guided herself towards the total darkness where she anticipated the stairs would be.

After a final rub against her calves, the cat had mewed appreciatively and disappeared. Despite frequent pauses to listen, frozen against the cool wood of the banisters, she could detect no other sound of occupation in the building. She paused again now, feeling with her naked toes for the cold edge of linoleum beyond the carpet, and then for the glossy edge of the skirting board. Her left hand ran along the wall at her side, a slight rough feeling, as if it were distempered. She hesitated.

The obvious plan, said Cadbury to herself, is to find a bedroom and look for some clothes. Although the likelihood of detection, she added, is no doubt greatest there, too.

She moved forward slowly. Her hand slid over a sort of ridge, then a slight precipice, and onto a bumpy, smoother-textured surface. It felt like a door. Kneeling, she breathed deeply for a moment to gather her energy. She leaned her weight carefully against the architrave. It felt curiously reassuring to be crouched in a corner of something rigid and unmoving. She felt herself shiver.

Steady, girl, she said to herself. You're not as cold as you were. And the spiders have gone forever.

But the involuntary tremble convinced her of the need to find some covering. It was the sense of exposure rather than the cold that was making her feel under pressure. It might be a risk to go into the first bedroom that came to hand, but it was a risk that had to be taken.

Sliding her hands up the door, she felt for the knob, ran her fingers around it, and slowly, very slowly, began to turn it. It moved some distance and stopped. With a deep breath she rose to her feet, braced herself on the jamb, and firmly pushed. The door wouldn't budge.

Fuck, said Cadbury.

The next door proved equally recalcitrant. And the next. And the next. At the fourth door, Cadbury wiped the sweat from her brow along her thighs. She touched her belly and her breasts. She was wet with moisture all over.

If I don't get covered soon, she thought, I'll get pneumonia.

She remembered Valerian and his fetish about the cold. He would always maintain that the body was unusually sensitive to the germs of pneumonia after love-making, and would insist on the most rapid disengagement and scuttle for cover when the act had taken place in the open.

Stay a moment, love, she had said once on a beach in Devon, I haven't enjoyed the most of you yet.

But Valerian had unplugged himself and rolled under his trousers before replying.

One has to be careful, my sweet, he said. You'd be the first to complain if my cock froze off with the cold.

I should have thought it would make it more rigid.

Like a stalagmite.

Exactly, said Cadbury. Now pull your nice warm trousers on and come back inside me before you relax.

To be fair, she remembered, Valerian had done as he was bidden.

I'm sure that women's bodies are more resistant to cold than men's, he had said, stiffening to his task.

I keep mine furnace-fresh for the tempering of your naked blade, said Cadbury as she squirmed her buttocks in the sand.

But tonight she began to appreciate Valerian's sense of caution. After all, she had enjoyed the equivalent of more men than the Queen of Sheba with the Japanese vibrator. One could certainly say that she was exhausted after love-making, and thus unusually vulnerable to the cold.

This line of reminiscence and conjecture had the effect of soothing Cadbury's nerves. She pushed the hair from her eyes and bent to grip the fourth doorknob. It was the last on this side of the corridor, as she had already discovered by reaching out and touching a blank end wall with her knee. Her fingers took hold.

Before she began to turn, however, something strange about the darkness began to assert itself. There seemed to be a slight mist around her hand. With a quick movement, she bent and crouched. The small coffin shape of a keyhole, invisible on all the other doors, was brightly outlined before her eye. She moved forward and fitted her eye to the space.

There was a light on in the room. By it, she could see a fireplace, a wastepaper basket, and the back of a chair. There were no signs of present occupation, apart from the light, and no sounds, of voices, or water, or anything suggesting human habitation.

Cadbury thought for a moment. If, as seemed to be the case, there was no one in the room now, it looked as if someone would be returning soon. That meant that there would almost certainly be clothes available, but that they would have to be stolen fast. On the other hand, if there was someone sitting or lying quietly in the room, they would have to be dealt with.

She felt a sudden pang for the Japanese sword. Even the threat of that in the hands of a naked woman would probably be enough to shock any chance inhabitant into silence. Unless, of course, it was one of the crew, in which case she would have had to use it again. She felt a surge of adrenaline at the thought. The desire for righteous killing was infectious.

She dug her nails in her palms. There was no choice. Naked and unarmed as she was, she had to go into this room and get what she needed. By whatever means were demanded.

Gently, she turned the doorknob. Resting for a moment, she took a deep breath, coiled herself into a ball, thrust violently forward, and rolled in a tight bunch through the door and into the room. She was on her feet, spinning, reaching for a vase from the mantel above the fire, turning, swinging it up rim out as a weapon to go for someone's eyes, feet bracing to get her balance and still poised to dodge, if need be, all within a fraction of a second, while her eyes raced over the structure and furniture of the small bedroom she found herself in.

It was empty.

She turned towards the bathroom. Two strides and a quick glance made it clear that that was empty, too. And then a flood of relief swept through her. Lying on the cork bath mat, in a slight haze of steam, as if someone had just taken a bath, was a heap of discarded clothes.

He's nipped out for a shit, thought Cadbury. I'll have to be quick.

But it wasn't he. Bending to pick up the clothes, her fingers stubbed on a pair of child's heavy brogues, long black stockings, a garter-belt, a pair of navy-blue school knickers, and a small beautiful silver kimono patterned with the same leaves of the wild ginger plant as Yoshimitsu's had been.

The kimono for his daughter, she said. It must be her room.

Rapidly, she began to dress herself in the little girl's clothes, aware once more of that strange sense of her own past as she felt the familiar touch of the childhood materials on her skin. Firmly, she put the thoughts behind her.

The knickers were no problem. The rough woollen feel was attractive, and the tightness just short of indecency. The girl was obviously big for her age, since the stockings also slid up her legs without much trouble, and the click of the garter-clasps hooked them firmly in place. The kimono was extremely short, and it bulged with a positively obscene curvaceousness around Cadbury's copious hips. But it did close and fasten with the broad band of the obi at her waist. And the shoes, appallingly tight though they were, gave her feet a measure of protection.

Cadbury looked at herself in the steamed-up mirror, wiping

a space clean with her hand. She drew her eyes into narrow slits with her fingers.

I wouldn't let *you* go out with my son, she said.

The effect, she thought, was surprisingly adequate. It gave her an exotic charm.

As Cadbury looked at herself in the mirror, a slight noise disturbed her. Instinctively, she nudged the bathroom door to, and slid in the catch. Bending to the keyhole, she was aware that the door in the other room had opened, and there were light swishing movements. The long sweep of a man's kimono passed into her tiny space of vision. There was a creak, perhaps someone sitting down on the bed or a chair, then the sound of voices. The sounds were muffled, but it was clear that they were speaking Japanese. A second man had joined the other. Something else, to Cadbury's ears more encouraging, began to be apparent. The voices grew softer. There was a punctuation now of creaks and grunting sounds. In the narrow slit of the keyhole a hairy male leg came into view, then, as it turned, the firm pole of an erect male organ.

Cadbury licked her lips. It was a pity they were not on friendly terms. She withdrew her eyes with regret when she saw a hand gently stroke the foreskin to and fro. From the look of things, they were well under way, and she had perhaps less time than she would have liked.

The bathroom window, like the bedroom ones, was of a rounded Victorian sash type, held down by a stiff but movable catch. Cadbury eased it back. She reflected on the rapidity of her recovery. There couldn't be much wrong if she was anxious to have a man's prick in her mouth again already. She smiled to herself as the window slid up and she eased her leg over the sill.

She paused to look down. She was facing out across the harbor, towards the dark bulk of the moored submarine. Below her, there was the shadow of a long flat surface, perhaps the roof of a porch verandah. At any rate, it was a safe and easy drop. Dangling by her arms, she let herself go.

As Cadbury landed on soil below the verandah window, she glanced sharply to her left. A road led up in that direction into what looked like an avenue of trees. It must be the way to go. Edging along the house again, as she had done before, she reached the front porch. Ahead of her, there was darkness. She took a deep breath and ran.

The school brogues were awkward on her feet, and they seemed to make a colossal noise when their leather soles hit the ground. She half tripped, and crouched listening under a laurel bush. She was aware of something through another sense. There was a smell of gasoline. She followed her nose towards it. There, parked just off the road, was the bulk of a car.

Cadbury tried the door. It opened, and she slipped into a long low seat as the door clicked to. Her fingers slithered about, searching for the ignition. The keys were still in. Without thinking, she flicked the starter, swung the wheel, and revved out with a scrunch of tires into the road. As the headlights came on under her questing hands, and the car raced into second and third, she was aware of driving something fast, and of why it must have been there. They had obviously used this car to deliver the swords to the submarine, and it had been left ready for a quick getaway.

Nothing happened. And nothing happened still as she swept around what seemed to be a highly stylish small village, in a grand eighteenth-century style, with a dome and colonnades, and then up past an elaborate Victorian mansion, flickeringly shown up by the headlights, and finally out on a main road and away towards a signpost for Bangor.

Portmeirion, said Cadbury aloud. It must have been Portmeirion.

She pressed her foot hard down in her school shoes, and the GTE went up to ninety in fourth.

I can ditch this conspicuous and highly unsuitable vehicle, and travel, as a good schoolgirl should, by train, she reflected. And if Chester is still offering the sort of service it used to, I shall get to London in time for a late dinner.

She glanced at the brightly lit circle of the dashboard clock. The hands showed half past six. It was midway through the hour of the cock.

16

The bodies of the two Japanese lay prone at the edge of the pool. The severed heads, with the eyes staring forward as if still alive, stood upright on the wet stone. The darkness of the buildings and the rippling water was broken by the savage flicker of naked flame. All around the pool, facing the bodies and the figure of Yoshimitsu behind them, the crew of the submarine stood at attention, each man holding a blazing torch in his right hand. As the wind hissed in the trees and an occasional spatter of rain fell, the old man began to speak. His words were caught and carried by the wind, and the men with the torches tuned their ears so as not to miss them.

Three of our number are now dead, he said, stepping forward between the bodies. Tadashi Soko by his own hand in Gibraltar, preserving his honor out of the failure of his mission. Masahiro and Yoshida are here before you, their blood still hardly dry from the blow that killed them.

One of the men shifted, easing the weight of the resined

branch in his fingers. His long gray kimono fell open. Underneath he was wearing only a pair of black swimming trunks.

The woman who did this is no longer with us, the old man continued. You all heard the acceleration of the car a few moments ago. There is no way we can follow and bring her back. It is not important. In the venture to which we are all freely committed, there is no possible setback that can result in defeat. The deaths of our comrades are a momentary intermission. Tonight there are two more things to be done. Celebrate their funeral in fire, water, and air. And prepare our minds for the sea.

Pausing, he raised both hands in the air. The muscles in his forearms tensed, and the men around the pool fell to their knees. There was a moment's complete silence, broken only by the crackle of wood burning, and the gentle lap of the ripples. Then, one at a time, each man rose to his feet, slowly walked to the end of the pool, and touched the open eyes of the dead samurai with his free hand. As he did so, he leaned over and quenched the flame of his torch in the water. No sound broke the ritual silence except the hiss of dying fire and the sudden spurts of the wind. As each man returned to his place, and the light slowly died away, the water became full of floating branches, black and dead in the occasional rain. The set eyes of the kneeling Japanese fixed on their steady movement in a simple meditation on the passing speed of life.

When the last torch had been dipped in the water, and the complete darkness of extinguished light fell on their faces, the old man again began to speak.

Keep silent for a moment in the darkness, he said. The spirits must have time to settle in the water.

As he knelt on the slippery marble the old architect had completed his folly with, Yoshimitsu schooled his body to resist the pressures of the night. He felt cold and stiff, his knees bruised by the stone through the thin material of his kimono.

I must be firm, he thought while his eyes accustomed themselves to the dark and picked out the humped figures of his comrades around the pool. They depend on me.

Over their shoulders, he allowed himself to imagine the outlines of the dome and the church tower, the little eighteenth-century houses and the famous colonnade of Bath. He remembered his last visit to this exquisite survival as a member of a trade mission in the late nineteen-fifties. There had been less here then, but the principle had been the same. To hold the onslaught of the present in check. To restore the glory of an age of sanity.

Perhaps theirs was shorter than ours, he thought. But it was something. And Clough Williams-Ellis knew it.

He recalled the story of the young architect looking for a strip of land to build his private fantasy on, his discovery of the bay of Portmeirion, his purchase and development of it, and his successful attempt to preserve and retain its privacy. Where else in the world could he and his friends, the spiritual descendants of the forty-seven ronin, recoup and intensify their pride and sense of the past before the next stage in their mission? And where else could he celebrate the birthday of the little daughter he had bred from the loins of a Welsh servant girl, the one forgotten heir of his accumulated fortune. He shrugged the image away.

We have the swords, he thought. Do we have the will?

He smiled to himself as he thought of the English girl. In a way he was glad she had gone. She confirmed his sense of pride in the occasional lasting energy of the primitive virtues. She was fit to have been the mistress of Hideyoshi, a creature of feline elegance and brutality. As clear and decisive as the blade of the sword she had killed his comrades with. There was no dishonor in dying by such a cut as that. She had swung the sword like an expert executioner. The *kami* must have come to her aid.

Learn from the girl, he said to himself. Learn from the girl. She, too, was fit to be my daughter.

It seemed appropriate to think of her riding to London in the body of a Scimitar, free and invulnerable, like the hard steel in the core of a blade.

The wind stirred the floating logs, and they clonked together gently in the water. The dead eyes and the living stared as one.

The old man remembered his apprenticeship as a kitchen boy in the Imperial household before the First World War. He recalled the incident of the crayfish. The new cook had ordered a special consignment of three hundred exceptional crayfish from Hokkaido for the Coronation banquet in 1914. They had arrived alive and healthy and been accommodated in a deep tank of fresh water in the kitchen.

Crayfish, the little boy had said to himself as he leaned over the side and looked down at the slowly moving antennae, the questing bodies and the stiff armor-plated look of their heads.

A constant supply of fresh water had played on the crayfish from an overhanging pipe. Night and day the little boy had watched this stream of water enter and drain away from the tank. He had been fascinated by the endless flowing, and by the steady uneasy movement of the crustaceans as they reached up and fell away from their one source of sustenance and freedom. Sometimes a big one would succeed in clutching the edge of the pipe and hanging on, fighting to fix its grip before the rush of the water stripped it off and flung it back into the tank.

It was the night before the banquet that the little boy could bear it no longer.

After all, he thought, it would make no difference. How could they escape? One or two perhaps would make their way up into the cistern. But the rest would remain. And who would ever know?

Very slowly, he turned the tap. Until the water was a slow trickle. Until it came to a dripping stop.

In the tank, the three hundred crayfish from Hokkaido crawled to and fro. For a time they seemed quite unaware of any change in their environment. The cool incoming stream was perhaps so weak that they scarcely noticed it.

And then, suddenly, there seemed to be a curious restlessness in the tank. While the little boy watched, one after another a group of particularly large crayfish reached up and flickered a speculative claw at the pipe. Then one, the biggest of the lot, reached out, and took hold.

The little boy fled from the kitchen and up to his bed.

The next morning, Yoshimitsu remembered, no one could understand it. It seemed like a miracle. An adverse miracle. All three hundred crayfish had been spirited away in the darkness. Not a single one remained to explain what had happened. Some anti-Imperial thief had entered by stealth and extracted the lot.

The kitchen was a whirlwind of activity. What was to be done? It was too late to find another three hundred crayfish. The reputation of the chief cook was at stake. Visions of seppuku and lasting disgrace loomed up before him.

The little boy slipped away from the melee and crept up to the cistern. There, clambering out over the side, he found the last and smallest of the crayfish.

Look, he called. I've found one up here in the cistern.

At once, a full-scale search was set in train. And one by one, every single crayfish was discovered and restored to the tank. Some came from the cupboards under the sink, some from the corners of the larder. One had hidden itself in a tea caddy, one under a case of knives. Not a single one had been lost entirely.

As the last of the three hundred was restored to the tank, the chief cook sent for the little Yoshimitsu.

Good boy, he said. That was truly an inspiration of yours. To think of looking in the cistern. I shall see you are well rewarded for this.

So the three hundred crayfish were all boiled and eaten. Not one escaped. And the little boy who had let them out kept his mouth shut and was rewarded with rapid and instant promotion.

Perhaps there was a moral in that somewhere, thought Yoshimitsu as he watched the black charred wood roll and heave in the pool.

Friends, he said quietly in the darkness, it is time to prepare for the voyage. We must come together to a mutual understanding in the water. Prepare for it.

A gust of wind whipped the flank of his kimono open. Cold air stroked the hair on his thighs. He reached out and rested his hands on the two skulls to his left and right.

Farewell, friends, he said, and lifted himself to his feet, shedding the kimono in a long sweep. After pausing a moment, he dived headfirst among the floating branches, the splash of his body like a signal that echoed around the pool.

One after another, the others rose. There was the sound of swishing silk all around the pool. Then a steady succession of splashes, thuds, and slaps as the hard muscle and flesh of the samurai struck the water.

Yamaka remembered the girl as he loosened the obi at his waist. The last time he had swum had been with her. He explored his mixed feelings as he dived. The tenderness. And the rage. The ease with which she had dissolved into a man in his fantasies. The excitement and horror when he had run the vibrator over her groin, watching her squirm and mouth her extravagant obscenities as the jolt of the electric climaxes tore through her body.

His head went under and he held his breath as he swooped under the water in the icy cold. Coming up, blowing for air, he tasted the bitterness of burned wood in his mouth. Fragments of charred elm were on his tongue. Around him, the bodies of his friends smote and charged the pool. He trod water, knifing his legs open and shut as he felt the familiar throb start in his belly.

A hand slid over the bulge in his trunks. He pretended

to fight free, allowing the exploring invisible fingers to control and master his resistance. Another pair of hands was under his armpits, gently sliding over his taut nipples from behind. A hairy chest brushed his belly as he surrendered to a whirlwind of excitement, and reached out for whatever his hands could reach.

Everywhere there were the plundering gasps and breathless coughings of a large congregation in desperate physical engagement. In the darkness, man met man in anonymous loving grip, caressing or violent, full of the necessary absolution and expenditure of shame that their self-commitment required.

Ieyasu, someone gasped. Ieyasu. Ieyasu.

The word seemed to be taken up all around the pool, mingling with the male noises and the wind's hiss.

Ieyasu. Ieyasu.

It seemed to work like the onset of a mass climax. As Yamaka stirred and rolled in the water, kneading and kneaded by what seemed a thousand hands, he felt the gum of his whole being stiffen and melt into the final channels of expression.

Ieyasu, he gasped. O Ieyasu.

The word squeezed at his belly. With a last thrust, he expended his body in a stream of jetting intensity. He felt a hot rush of liquid over his own face, across his calves. Wood and wet silk, burning and cold, all seemed to mix in a terrible final communion of the earth, the body, and the air.

Half-drowned, he dragged himself towards the side, hauled his dripping limbs up onto the stone. Around him, the others lay or crawled as he had done, exhausted and at one.

For Yoshimitsu, handled and thrown to and fro as he had not been since his distant indecent youth, it was as if he had become one of his own lost and discovered crayfish, renewed, expended, and reimprisoned. Made one with each other, and made ready for the sea. And for the final banquet of the flesh in Israel.

Feeling his old knotty limbs twitch into their orgasm, under the exploring hands of whoever had reached him last, he withdrew his body with a great heave, and flung himself back towards the headless bodies on the brink. Kneeling between them with his need in his own hands, he shook out what few drops of annealing sperm he could over the cold severed heads he had recruited and caused to be killed.

Be with us still, he murmured in the darkness as he collapsed, worn out, between their bodies.

Minutes later, when the cold wind began to make them feel their exposure more keenly, Yoshimitsu spoke again aloud.

Take their bodies back to the ship, he said.

Four naked men ran forward and lifted the corpses to their shoulders. Two more came forward and gently lifted the heads.

As Yoshimitsu led the way, they began to sing. All together, walking in a solemn procession, soaked in sperm and wood-fragmented water, back to their submarine, they sang an old Japanese folk song, remembered from their childhood. Tears started in their eyes in the darkness as their bare feet crunched over the grit and the earth back through the beautiful false eighteenth-century paradise an English architect had created for his own pleasure to their private modern world of steel and rubber ready to plunge below the sea towards slaughter and dominion.

The wind brought more rain, whipping their faces. And it was the hour of the dog.

THE HOUR OF THE DOG
8:00 P.M.

17

The train moved with its lulling, familiar rhythm through the darkness. Through the long window, streaked with occasional dotted lines of rain, Cadbury stared out at the floating reflection of herself in the night. With a sort of strange narcissism, she admired the soft fall of her combed yellow hair over the gleaming silver of her kimono, the creamy skin of her upper thigh where the kimono fell back above the dark sheen of the stockings. She allowed her hand to stray into the fork of her legs, shook back the folds of the silk and watched her reflected fingers play on the outline of her *mons Veneris* beneath the elastic-edged school knickers.

I wonder why trains always excite me, she thought, easing the tight elastic from her waist and allowing the puckered furrow of her navel to show.

On an impulse, she stood up and pressed her belly against the window, enjoying the sudden cold on her naked skin. She pressed her face to the glass, feeling the coolness over her nose and her eyelashes. She opened her mouth, rubbed her lips on the lips of the strange transparent schoolgirl who faced her, allowed her tongue to come out and lick the bitter taste of the glass.

I want you, she said to herself. I want you.

She parted her thighs, feeling the elastic of the knickers tense almost to bursting point. Her lower body leaned forward, and she felt the cold, exciting shock of the glass where her stripped sex went forward and met the sex of her partner, her reflection, her own self.

My little sister, she murmured. I love you so much.

Afterwards, as she lay back on the coarse moquette of the window seat, watching the remote lights of a town flick by, she breathed deeply in contentment.

Her mind ran back over the events of the past few hours. Since reaching Chester, and abandoning the Scimitar over a double yellow line near the station, she had enjoyed unusual good fortune. The next through train to London had been due in five minutes, and she had managed to hover by the barrier and slip through just as the guard was blowing his whistle.

Here, the porter on the gate had called. You can't do that.

I have, darling, she had replied, with a cheerful wave, pulling herself onto the moving train.

Very choice, the guard remarked as he admired the outlines of her disappearing thighs. Very choice indeed.

They just don't care, said the porter, with a shake of his head. Mine are just the same.

They'll make her pay in London, said the guard as they watched the train receding.

But Cadbury had heard none of this. She had walked down the corridor until she came to an empty compartment with a window seat facing the engine and a No Smoking sign on the window. There she had settled herself to rest and think, fairly sure that she could get by without attracting too much attention until the train reached Paddington. She had chosen to travel first class, and the compartments were all fairly empty. When the ticket collector came around, if he did, she anticipated some trouble, but nothing that her female charm would find beyond its compass. There were compensations in being a woman, she reflected as she eased her bottom on the seat and leaned her head back on the white linen rest.

She felt very tired, and her thoughts began to stray towards those places she always kept them from. She remembered her father again in the little semidetached house in Otterburn, remembered coming home from school with her satchel and her blazer, and the frail thin old man serving her toast and Madeira cake. She remembered the warm North Country sitting room, with a blazing log fire in the grate, and her chair drawn up close so that she felt the heat on her bare knees. She remembered the sweet taste of the black-currant jelly, and the irritation of the unmended cane against the backs of her legs. And then her father's voice.

What happened today, Jane?

And the little girl who had later become Cadbury would go into her complex mixture of truths and untruths, the tale of her hopes and fears reassembled and unrolled to give her father the pleasure and reassurance he needed.

I shan't be here always, you know.

Those terrible words had been spoken a hundred times, but it was the hundredth she always remembered. The cold November rain against the bay window. A bedraggled terrier running for home across the road. And the slow ticking of the wag-clock she would have to sell in a few weeks at auction.

I shan't be here always, you know.

And then the unbearable groaning in the night. Her inability to help with the pain. The doctor coming with his serious face the next morning. And the ride to the hospital in the back of the ambulance.

The tears came again now in Cadbury's eyes as she remembered, and the little girl in the window of the train cried with her.

And as she cried, Cadbury cried herself to sleep. Leaning with her golden hair on the streaming glass against the reflection of her silver kimono, she began to dream. Everything that she had obscurely felt about her own identity, her deep love for her dead father, and her commitment to the Service under Loyola, broke and dissolved into a mess of sensations where truth and fantasy were inextricably mixed.

Once again, she bent above the tensed thin face of her dying father in the ambulance. Only this time she bent with her lips parted and her shoulders trembling. Her mouth opened and closed on his, and she felt his long weak arms come out from under the blankets and pull her body down.

My daughter, he whispered. My daughter.

While they lay together, naked and loving, in the moving metal room, it was another man who was parting the soft flesh in her groin. On the black plastic, as it now was, the old man with the rounded spectacles was unbuttoning his fly.

My daughter, he whispered as the taxi lurched on a corner. My daughter.

She tilted her face back, allowing her tongue to work out and lick the corners of his eyes. She felt the slippery silk of his kimono against the hardening tips of her nipples.

Ieyasu, she gasped. Ieyasu.

There were more lights outside the window now, and Cadbury woke with a start, drying her eyes on the child's handkerchief. They would soon be in London.

From down the corridor she heard the sound of a door opening and closing, then another. And then a more disturbing sound.

Tickets, please.

It was still several compartments away, but the collector was working closer.

Fuck it, said Cadbury, the dream disappearing in her mind.

She was not in the mood for the mixture of ingenuity and seduction necessary to get away without trouble. An idea struck her. It was just possible that she could win some time by a trip to the lavatory, slip out when the conductor had gone past, and then drop off the train in the outskirts of London before it pulled in.

With a quick movement, she reached the compartment door, looked through, made sure the corridor was empty, and slipped out. She walked quickly in her heavy brogues to the end of the corridor and reached the door of the toilet. It was engaged.

Fuck it again, said Cadbury.

She walked quickly down the length of the next corridor.

This time there was no toilet. She was about to go farther when she saw a man swaying down the corridor towards her. He paused and entered a compartment.

He was probably the man in the loo, she thought. I'll take a chance.

She ran back along the corridor and reached the door of the lavatory. It was unlocked. With a sigh of relief, she pushed it open and entered.

The door slammed shut behind her, and the bolt was run in. A man faced her in the tiny room. He was wearing a peaked cap and carried a punch and a notebook.

Where's your ticket, little girl, he said.

His breath smelled foul in her face.

I haven't got one, she said. Let me out of here. I'll explain why.

Oh, I can't do that, said the man, with a slow smile. I'll have to keep you in custody.

He seemed quite old, about fifty-five, with a drooping gray mustache and spectacles. He looked momentarily harmless, and Cadbury's guard was down.

I only meant to hide, she said. And I needed a pee. Honestly I did. I'd have offered to pay at Paddington. I just felt afraid when I heard you come down the corridor.

Even as she spoke, she realized that something was wrong. The collector had put down his punch and book in the washbasin, and had begun to unbutton his trousers.

Dear me. Dear me, he said. We'll have to be punished for that now, won't we?

Cadbury brought her knee up in a rapid movement towards the man's groin.

You dirty old bugger, she said.

The image of his hot sperm flooded through her, oozed out and over her thighs. She backed away, dragged the door open, stumbled out into the corridor.

The train had slowed. It was running through a large city. They must be nearly at Paddington. She ran to the door, swung it open in the rain and wind. It slammed back, swung open again, as she lowered herself towards the rails and jumped.

18

Valerian sat with his back to the wall. The candle on the table in front of him flickered occasionally as one of the young men went by with a plate of food, and he enjoyed the shadows of the other diners thrown up on the white-washed walls of the restaurant. Valerian rarely ate alone, and when he did he tended to choose somewhere dark, where he could be anonymous. Julie's was his favorite.

The reason for this self-imposed solitude was a double one. Valerian was still shaken by his tea with Loyola, and he needed time to think. He also needed time to read, and a quiet evening by himself with a nicely cooked trout seemed the best way to get this.

With almonds, he had said to the waiter, and he regarded it now with pleasure as it was set before him. The waiter himself would have appealed, too, he reflected, had it not been for his daunting recollections of Angeline. There was a hint of excessive puissance about the young man's closely fitting tweeds.

I'll bet he's wearing French knickers, thought Valerian. And a size too small.

The young man's eyes looked up with a cold indifference when he withdrew his hand from the plate. These middle-aged heteros were a pain in the arse, in his opinion.

Will that be all, sir, he said.

His cheesecloth shirt was a button farther undone than convention prescribed, and he gave Valerian a glimpse of the curling hair on his nipple.

Very tasty, said Valerian, and turned to his food with anticipation.

I hope your cock drops off, said the young man, but he said it under his breath. The manager was resistant to bad manners, and even more to the provoking of violence. And Valerian, he reflected, looked perfectly capable of that. If of nothing else, he added to himself to soothe his vanity.

Valerian squeezed the slice of lemon over the delicately burned surfaces of the fish. He sniffed appreciatively, and took a long draught of his white wine. It was Italian, dry, and very cold. The long, pinched-in bottle lay on its side in a bucket of crushed ice to his right.

I wonder where she is, he thought.

For a long time Valerian had known how important Cadbury was, and this was something that he knew he must keep from Loyola. The Service was very hard on cases of emotional involvement. There had been the man discovered in the sewer at Greenwich, for instance. Valerian put his fork down. He didn't want to remember the man at Greenwich.

Testicles are for the Service was one of Loyola's favorite maxims. About as tasty and useful as sweetbreads. The heart is a form of offal. It does for the pig's trough.

But Valerian knew there were other uses for the heart. In his case, it was something he had no more absolute control of than the quivering in his stomach when it confronted rice or porridge.

Let's hope she's alive, he thought.

For a moment, the appetite had left him, and he dabbed at his lips with a paper napkin.

He felt a strange sad shivering inside him at the thought of all that yellow hair and those beautiful empty gray eyes reduced to earth or ashes.

Don't let her die, he murmured, with his eyes on the Christian fish. Don't let her die.

Valerian's hand strayed to the little pile of books and magazines on the seat beside him. He allowed his fingers to close on the glossy wrapper of a small, squarish book, and lifted it onto the table beside the candle. As the flame guttered in the socket, he eased the book open, and turned to the place he had remembered.

The *kanji* for suffering, he read to himself, is *mon* or *moda(eru)*. It is written as a gate with the heart enclosed inside it.

Valerian studied the flowing lines of the Chinese character in the flicker of the candle flame. There was perhaps no way out, only the mind locked in its own tensions and struggling to be free.

He pushed the trout away from him. His appetite had for the moment entirely gone, and he reached out for another drink of the wine. At least that might help to dull his feelings.

As he lifted the glass to his lips, a slight easing seemed to come in his heart. He closed his eyes while he drank, enjoying the cool flowing over his tongue.

Would you like the trolley, sir, said a voice.

Not yet, replied Valerian as his eyes opened. Not yet. Sit down a moment first.

She was wearing a long leather overcoat, and her hair was tangled over her shoulders. Those empty gray eyes were fixed on him, and she was smiling a crooked smile. She was alive, and she was Cadbury, and he loved her. And the world was back to normal.

So tell me why you're so late, he added. I mean, it doesn't exactly help if you turn up three whole days after time. And how did you know where I was, anyway?

Where else would you be, said Cadbury.

It's good, she continued as she reached out and nibbled

the trout. I can see you've finished with it. I'll help myself.

With a sensuous movement, she heaved the coat off her shoulders onto the back of the seat.

My Christ, said Valerian. You'll get me arrested. Why on earth are you going about in a rumpled kimono?

I was nearly raped by a ticket collector, said Cadbury simply, and she plucked the bottle of wine from the ice and tipped it obscenely into her mouth.

The young man was hovering in an ecstasy of embarrassment.

Is the young lady eating, sir, he inquired.

Just practicing her fellatio in public, said Valerian. But we'll see in a minute. So just fuck off and leave us alone, would you?

It wasn't his day, the waiter reflected. He would have that ancient bastard's balls if it was the last thing he did.

Over a liberal helping of profiteroles, Cadbury completed her account of her adventures. She had by that time disposed of an avocado with shrimps, an underdone steak with spinach, most of another bottle of white wine, and a brace of hard rolls with butter. Valerian had watched in amused relief, contenting himself with an occasional nibble at the wreck of his trout. Shock had eased his worries, but not restored his appetite.

So finally, she said, licking cream off her lips, I picked myself off the track with no more than a handful of bruises, so far as I could feel, and headed for the station. I was able to rip off this jokey little bit of top dressing in the Superloo, and from there it was easy. I think the taxi driver thought I was some kind of les act out on the rampage.

Anyway, he let me off with a feel of his balls and a promise to have dinner tomorrow with his wife's cousin in Balham.

You'll be missing that, said Valerian. I'll tell you why. But later. I suggest we go. And have coffee at your flat.

With cream and with sugar, said Cadbury, and with all the accessories.

Later, they lay together smoking on Cadbury's double bed, with Alexis across their legs. Rain pattered on the window in the darkness, and they drew silently on the sweet relaxing smoke. The dog growled as they stirred. He had been well fed, and he was happy his mistress was back. He wanted to sleep and enjoy himself.

They had come in and collapsed on each other, after a brief pause to disorientate the bugging system with a long-playing tape of hard rock on the hi-fi. The school knickers and the stockings had revived Valerian's flagging desire, and he had taken her without preliminaries.

You dirty bugger, she had gasped. You're just like that fucking ticket collector.

Just? said Valerian as he stripped her kimono back. In every possible way?

Only worse, she panted. Your prick's bigger. And it's going to hurt like shit. My Christ, she gasped, and Valerian had rammed himself clean into her to the hilt.

It had been a release for Valerian, and he lay at ease in the darkness. But he felt the Furies not far away, and a cold sweat kept coming and going on his body.

Are you cold, love, said Cadbury.

Not cold, said Valerian. Just thinking about the *kanji*

for loyalty. It's like a heart with a dagger in it from above. I imagine that Loyola would like it.

He reached up to switch the light on, and swung his legs to the ground. The dog growled angrily. What kind of behavior was this on his mistress's bed?

Look, said Valerian, and he drew the character on a page of his diary.

And what's the character for love like, said Cadbury, leaning on his bare shoulder.

Like this, said Valerian as he drew again. Like a paddy field on a heart.

Like a hot cross bun on a heart, said Cadbury. And a bun in the oven is what it often leads to.

Valerian had gone to the window, and was looking out at the rain on the glass.

Poor Loyola, he said. A heart with a dagger in it, that's all he gets for his pains.

He thought back to those last few minutes of his tea that afternoon. He remembered the pouting, spoiled face above the plate of cake as the terrible story had been slowly revealed.

You see, Loyola had said, glancing down at his hands, there is a touch of *Machtpolitik* about all this. We knew about the proposed rising and the assassination plot all along. Ever since Yoshimitsu Tokugawa, dear old love, came in to see us at Branch 9 one day last year. The Department of Trade and Industry was very keen on his proposition, of course. Even the P.M. quite liked it, bless him.

Valerian remembered hearing the wind shriller in the elms, and feeling a dryness in his throat.

The proposition was, continued Loyola, that the British government should finance and support a right-wing isolationist coup in Japan by conniving at the transfer, by legal, and in some cases rather less legal, means, of a substantial number of samurai swords. The inducement, of course, being our trade interests. As you know, the Nips have been really biting into our markets overseas for many years, and the thought of a cut in the number of export Mitsubishi products was very enticing. If Yoshimitsu and his boys came to power, they promised a return to the grand old isolationism of the eighteenth century.

Valerian had gagged on his chocolate cake and listened.

Did the government actually pledge its support, he had asked.

He remembered Loyola's gravely inclined head and his saddened nod.

I fear they did, old boy. I fear they did. You see, he seemed so plausible, and so rich. It took some considerable research to establish that there was very little of a back-up operation on his home ground. We were tempted. I confess it, and we were deceived.

He had reached out for more of the lemon-meringue pie.

However. It is now clear that we have been let down by Yoshimitsu and his shining knights in armor. They have no more chance of success with their coup than a hive of wasps in a jar of treacle. I have already alerted the Israelis that the assassination is not to take place.

You mean they'd agreed to connive at it?

Loyola had licked crumbs from his fingers.

Indeed they had, he had said. They had little choice. You see, the Americans dropped a word in their ear about military aid.

And the Americans, too, are now pulling the carpet out from under the coup?

As firmly and as quickly as we are, said Loyola.

As he lay feeling Cadbury's beautiful thigh warm on his hip, Valerian wondered if he should have told her all this. He shivered. It was too late. He heard the tape grind to its end.

I want you both to go out and wind things up, Loyola had concluded. There seems no need to bother the Israelis with the *coup de grâce*. They would very much rather turn a blind eye. And you may feel it rather fun to complete the affair yourselves.

A steely glint had come into his eyes.

After all, you perhaps feel that you owe these little yellow bastards a lesson. I'm sure that Cadbury does. I suggest a Lewis gun on the tarmac. You'll adore that sensual shuddering.

They were both lying in the darkness again, and Alexis was breathing heavily at their feet.

Do you think they're really going to do it, said Cadbury.

You know them a good deal better than I do, said Valerian. But I think they are. I think they really are.

Then we'd better get some sleep, said Cadbury, and she curled herself into Valerian's side. The dog rolled in his doze, and licked her knee through the single sheet that covered them. It was still the hour of the dog, but it was nearly over.

The Hour of the Wild Boar

10:00 p.m.

19

The young man bent under the raised hood to keep his head out of the rain. Leaning his belly on the car, he reached in to unscrew the close-fitting steel cap of the crankcase. His fingers turned the cap with the practiced skill of an expert mechanic, and his eyes ran lovingly over the Ferrari's engine. A gust of wind carried drops of water onto the black surface of the long air cleaner above the triple-bodied carburetors, and he paused to brush it with the back of his dungaree sleeve.

Christ, I'd like one of these, he thought.

Cadbury lay back in the worn leather driving seat, and watched him through the glass. She had cut the electric wipers, and the rain was beginning to blur the image again. He was a good-looking boy, even if a bit conceited. And he was taking care while he poured. She liked that.

I'll take a piss, said Valerian, beside her. The bastard looks as if he's going to be all night with that oil.

He opened the door, flooding the car with light and cold air, and then cutting both off again when he swung it to and ran across the yard towards the lavatory, folding up his collar against the rain.

Cadbury's eyes swung back to the young man. In the rain

and darkness on their way to the airport, there was something exquisitely exciting about this temporary pause. Her senses had settled into an acute alertness, drinking in and storing up every detail of the surrounding sensuous world. She enjoyed the faint smell of leather and tobacco in the car, the slight stickiness of the seat on the backs of her thighs, the little creaks as she changed her position. In front of her the luminous dials shone, providing their information about fuel and oil pressure, speed and revolutions per minute, as surely as the stars glittering in the sky above London.

Ten o'clock, she said aloud to herself as her eye caught the automatic clock. There's time and to spare.

She unclicked the door and stepped out onto the concrete, holding her arms to herself to keep in the warmth.

The young man watched her long legs emerge into the rain and the wind. He lifted the oil can and shook it, holding it well away from the gleaming blue of the car's body. He spoke as he screwed the cap firmly back into place.

What have you had her up to?

Hundred and thirty, said Cadbury. There was plenty in hand.

The young man nodded. He believed her. She was the kind of woman he would like to have made a pass at, but the outside lavatory was hardly likely to detain her fancy man more than a minute or two.

Cadbury shivered as she stood looking down into the engine. The young man reached forward involuntarily to put his arm around her.

Here, you'll get cold, he said.

She smiled, and passed her hand quickly over his lips, then his eyes.

You're sweet, she said softly. I wish there was more time.

He held the car door for her and she climbed back in out of the cold.

Valerian zipped his trousers up and swung the loose wooden door open again. The wind gusted in, and he paused before making his dash back. As his eye took in the long rakish line of the Pinninfarina body, the drops of water gleaming on the slant of the roof, the mud flecking the wire wheels, with their knock-on racing hubs, he began to feel his depression lift a little. He had awakened after a disturbed night, and been unable to sleep again.

The dream, he had thought. The dream.

And the cold hand had begun to crawl in his bowels. It had been the usual, terrible dream he had had so many times since childhood, and never been able to explain or account for.

He was in a tall steel tube, about six or eight feet wide, without projections, and stretching up indefinitely to some invisible ceiling or top. There was no way of climbing up or digging down and out. Everything was perfect, finished, ice-cold metal.

And beside him was a dog. Barking. A small wire-haired terrier. Endlessly barking and barking.

Why this made him so afraid he could never tell. But he would wake sweating and screaming.

The young man waited as Valerian ran back towards the

pumps. The rain spurted and leaped from the puddles in the concrete as his shoes splashed and skidded.

Five quid for the petrol, he said flatly. Another forty for the oil.

Valerian felt for his wallet.

You've checked the water, he said.

They never need it, said the young man contemptuously.

But he had checked. He remembered the dull handsome pea-green of the antifreeze in the tank. And the small balls above the clear water in the battery. He had checked that, too.

And the tires, said Valerian.

I've given you thirty-two behind, twenty-eight in front, said the young man. A four-pound differential for the motorway. I can see your lady friend puts her foot down.

Valerian handed over a fiver and a pound note.

Keep the change, he said. And buy yourself a *Penthouse*.

Back in the car he closed his eyes. He was still very jumpy.

Away, James, he said. And don't spare the horses.

The famous Ferrari roar came back off the wall of the ramp up to the motorway when Cadbury changed into second and the tachometer flashed up to six thousand at fifty.

Better fasten your seat belt, she said. You were lousy to that kid.

A smaller swathe of the road lit up when she clicked the main beam off and the car shot across the double broken line onto the feed road. In the outside lane she went into third, and approached ninety. Ahead there were red lights, and she cut back into the inside lane and then out again past a Mercedes. His long horn followed them with a dwindling echo as the car's speedometer passed the hundred mark and began to climb to a hundred and ten.

Could you try the overdrive, shouted Valerian. It would help communication.

Cadbury smiled as the needle reached, and she held it at, a hundred and twenty. The engine roar dropped, and she let the car drive itself. At this speed it seemed to wake up, like a huge drowsy cat only slowly shaking a vast residue of sleep out of its limbs.

You're right, said Valerian. I'm sorry.

Cadbury's hand reached out and touched his knee. A shrill whine began in the car as the speedometer needle registered a hundred and twenty-five. The steady sweep of the wipers was clearing the rain and mud from the road, and Cadbury pressed the front and rear window blowers. At this speed with the windows up it would mist quickly.

Don't worry, poppadom, she said softly. We'll survive.

In the furious noise of the car's progress in the rain and darkness, Valerian began to unlock again. Being driven by Cadbury was like submitting one's sexuality to the demands of a nymphomaniac. The experience was total. But she was the best driver he had ever known, and he felt absolutely safe with her.

I've been thinking, he said.

As he spoke, he folded his knees up and tipped his spine a little forward, so that he sat as in the cinema, in the archetypal womb position. Outside the window, the occasional lights of suburban houses flashed and disappeared like comets.

If they don't alter their schedule, he continued, and if

they succeed in killing Takada tonight, we'll both be out of a job this time. We might stay on in Israel and organize a Christmas show for the troops.

Cadbury flickered her lights to clear a small sedan in the fast lane. When it swayed in, she lifted her hand in a two-finger sign.

If they kill Takada, she said, we shall both be dead. You know that as well as I do.

Valerian closed his eyes. He had a sudden vision of Loyola in his office, and of how his voice had changed under Angeline's expert fingers. He knew what Loyola would do.

There's no stopping Loyola, he said. He's a force of nature.

He watched the dashboard lights as the needle rose to a hundred and thirty-five. There was no stopping Cadbury either.

Under the heavy, crude concrete of the airport long-term parking lot, the cars threw long shadows over the oil-stained floor. There was a sound of steady dripping as water came in from the stanchions outside. An occasional footstep, or a burst of voices, broke the long, slow silence.

Cadbury sat back behind the wheel, her eyes closed. They had seemed to need this moment's complete break. Since their arrival five minutes ago, neither had made a move, or wanted to speak. It was as if the car formed their last safe protection against the bitter world of oncoming violence and tragedy they were both about to step out into.

They lay with their hands clasped, like a knight and his lady on a medieval tomb. All around, the exhausted and weary blocks of metal that had brought their contemporaries towards the point of departure steamed and sweated in the darkness. They were ready, and yet not quite ready, to go.

And then Orpheus looked round, said Valerian. And Eurydice was snatched away from him forever into hell.

Holding Cadbury's hand still, he reached out to unlock the car door, and pushed it open. Without looking at her, he released her hand and stepped out onto the concrete. As she opened her door and joined him, they smiled at each other.

We'll survive, poppadom, she said.

Twenty yards away, Loyola watched them from behind the wheel of his Mercedes. He had worked too long for the Service to be worried about what he was going to do. He eased his thick limbs in the constricting material of his suit. It was time.

Drawing on a pair of tight leather driving gloves, he opened the car door and stepped out. He walked slowly towards the agents he had trained and come to understand as well as any he had ever employed.

Hello, you two, he said.

Valerian turned. He could hear the drip of oil from a leak somewhere in a car. It wasn't water, he was sure. It sounded softer.

Loyola was dressed from head to foot in tight, fetishistic leather. Leather trousers, close to his thighs and calves all the way down, were laced with leather straps at his ankles. He wore a tight leather battle jacket, nipped in at the waist and bound at the wrists with leather straps. Around his waist was a broad leather belt, stretched to the limit, and from the belt hung the multiple thongs of a rawhide bullwhip.

Faint light gleamed on all the soft black surfaces of the leather, and the material creaked slightly as he moved.

Hello, Loyola, said Valerian.

Loyola ignored him. He spoke to Cadbury.

Unbutton your dress, he said.

She was wearing an ankle-length batik silk dress which buttoned all the way down. Loyola watched as her fingers slowly undid the buttons and the dress fell apart. Underneath it, she was naked.

I expected that, said Loyola.

Is this necessary, said Valerian.

Lie down on the car, Cadbury, said Loyola.

As she lay back on the trunk, the girl's breasts reared and glistened in the dim light. A slight river of sweat or rain flowed down from her neck through the channel between them towards her belly.

The other way up, said Loyola.

The girl rolled over so that the length of her naked body was spread out over the cool, wet metal.

Now lift your dress up over your bottom, said Loyola.

Valerian watched as in a dream while Cadbury's hands came down and fumbled up the silken material in tucked folds above the cleft of her buttocks. In spite of himself, he felt a sudden sharp stirring of sexual desire at the sight of her body stretched and lifted against the car.

Cadbury waited with her muscles tensed. She could feel the smooth hard paintwork below her belly, the pressure of the shaped rounded steel along the contours of her shoulders and over her thighs. There was a tingling chill along the backs of her naked legs, and her buttocks shivered into sudden goose flesh, partly from cold, partly from fear and

from a strange excitement at what was coming. She felt a
warm trickle of sweat between her thighs, and she slithered
a little on the car's body.

He's going to whip me, she thought. A shudder ran up
through her arms.

Valerian watched while Loyola reached down to his waist
and unloosed the whip. He swung it in the air and brought
it down on the concrete with a flashing crack. The report
echoed in the confined space.

This is the hour of the wild boar, said Loyola. Remember
it.

As he spoke he drew a sort of hood down over his head,
and to Valerian's horror he was suddenly dressed in the skin
of a pig. The brutal tusks curved away from short nostrils,
bristling with rough hair. Small beady eyes glared out above
the long, crudely molded nose.

Don't do it, Loyola, he said.

The first stroke exploded in her body like a shot of cocaine.
Her body shook and quivered along the car. She gripped her
lips together, desperate not to cry out. Her head wrenched
around while the long arm came up for its second lash.

You dirty pig, she whispered, her eyes dilating with shock
when she saw the thong in the hands of a beast.

This time the strands of the lash seemed to coil around
and linger in all the cells of her body. She felt herself
drenched in a kind of extravagant trembling.

No more, you pig, no more, she moaned as the pain
crawled like a nest of ants through her whole nervous system.

But the next stroke was an introduction to a world of
complex and mysterious horror. Her legs opened and she

rubbed her breasts along the metal as if the car itself were fucking her and torturing her at once.

You lousy pig, she screamed. I want to come.

Valerian looked down at the blood-streaked weals along the girl's back. The squirming of her bare legs had excited him almost beyond endurance. He had felt himself wanting to snatch the whip from Loyola's hand and ply it himself.

He knelt suddenly, vomiting on the concrete, as the lash stopped. All he could hear was the girl's sobbing, and the heavy breathing of the man in the pig mask.

Get up, said Loyola, thickly. His voice was twisted and distorted inside the mask.

Valerian rose, reeling slightly, and wiped vomit from his chin.

Button your dress, said Loyola to Cadbury.

The girl stood away from the car, fingering the small horn buttons back into their holes. He turned again to Valerian.

Take down your trousers, he said.

As Valerian lay face down on the car's trunk, he remembered a scene that had horrified him in a film he had once seen. Two tramps had stripped and raped a fat, middle-aged man in a wood, forcing his friend to watch at gunpoint as they did so. At least this was better than that.

He remembered floggings at school, and how he had once broken the record during his time as head prefect. He tensed his body to meet the first of the strokes, quivering along the hamstrings.

Cadbury watched as Loyola tucked the whip back into his belt. He walked up to Valerian, and looked down at him. Then he turned to her, and deliberately unzipped his fly.

Christ, no, she said. Not that.

The lewd pressure was between his legs a second after he realized his mistake. He retched at the feel of the heavy leather creature grotesquely spraddling his buttocks, the hot fetid warmth of the old body over his flesh. His arms were expertly pinned down, his legs forced wide as the strong even thrusts went in and out, in and out. Fucking him. Buggering him.

You're not bad for a virgin, said Loyola. Not bad at all.

As Cadbury watched, she realized for the first time exactly what the Service meant. She could have stepped forward and killed the beast on her lover's back with a single karate chop. She could no more have done so than she could have killed her own father.

Worse, she thought as she watched in fascination the squirming of Valerian's buttocks under the leather. It turns me on.

But for Valerian, as for his hero Lawrence, the shock and horror of discovering that he enjoyed it was more than his shaken faculties could stand. As the beast who was Loyola shuddered finally into its climax, jerking his body full of its gluey semen, Valerian lost consciousness for a moment, and the little death of his master was for him the obliteration of sensation.

———————

Have a good flight, said Loyola as he zipped his trousers up. He tossed the pig mask at their feet and walked away towards his Mercedes.

20

Outside, the full moon shone on the waves, expanding a trail of pale yellow from the horizon to the Rock of Andromeda. As the old man watched from the open window, he imagined the naked girl chained to the wet stone. It would hardly have been a warm autumn night, as now. Perhaps the rain would have been falling. His mind dwelt on her straggling soaked hair, her limp exhausted body, when the dragon appeared from the mist, all fire and smoke and slithering skin in the heart of the storm.

But in our art, you would only see a part of it, he mused aloud, fingering the forked tongue and the three claws on the *tsuba* of his *katana*.

The young Japanese looked out at the moon and nodded.

They must always have the whole thing, he said, with distaste. Never the suggestion, always the glutted whole. Even down to the boy Perseus arriving, with his little woman's tits and his etiolated penis.

The old man shifted his position, swinging the sword behind the long fall of his rich purple kimono.

Poor Burne-Jones, he said. We could have made something of him. Imagine that skill with figures on the lid of a *suzuribako!*

For them, said Yamaka, it would only have been a biscuit tin. They have no *kami.*

The old man grunted. For a long time he looked out at the mobile light on the water, endlessly shifting and re-forming along the basic line from the rock to the point where the sea met the sky and the darkness.

Are we any better, he said.

We shall be, replied Yamaka, and he let his fingers play along the gilded cock inlaid on his *kashira,* pecking forever for seeds on the black stippled ground near the fallen drum.

The two men stood in silence. It was an hour before midnight, and the thing they had come to Israel to do was still an embryo in the darkness.

Let's begin, said Yoshimitsu.

Three hours before, the submarine with its cargo of swords had surfaced a mile up the coast in a little bay where the Greeks had drowned their Jewish neighbors in 166 B.C. The forty-four surviving ronin had disembarked and brought the swords ashore in a boat, repacking them on a cart and pushing it laboriously up the hill into the old Arab quarter of Jaffa. While the submarine rode at anchor for servicing and refueling, they had stored their weapons in the converted mosque where Yamaka and Yoshimitsu now stood talking.

The building was in the typical Arab style of the old town, square stone walls with arches, and a series of small flowing domes, all merging imperceptibly into the surrounding buildings and streets. After the Israeli victory in 1948, in one of the bloodiest campaigns of the war, the Arabs had left, and the old town was burned to the ground. Twenty years later, in a new climate of opinion, it had been carefully rebuilt as an art center; each house and mosque became a restaurant or a jeweler's shop.

Downstairs, this particular shop was an expensive resort for the rich from Tel Aviv and Los Angeles, a paradise of chased silver necklaces and beaten rings, crafted and fashioned by one of the most successful of the surviving Arab metal-smiths. To his clients from the big cities, Abdullah was a man of gentle charm, an acceptor of the new world of Israeli dominion, and a merchant with a shrewd but reasonable eye for a profit. To his friends in the casbah, he was a loyal and dedicated worker for the day of change, when the scimitars would flow again along the beach, and the blood run out into the sea like juice from the rotten melons in the *souk*.

You may stay as long as you wish, he had said to the old Japanese, extending the multiple jade rings on his thick fingers. Our two countries are at one in pride. I trust your mission.

It will be to our mutual good, said Yoshimitsu, and he had touched the Arab on the shoulder. I swear it will.

Over their Turkish coffee, they had admired each other's metalwork, and the expected bonds had been sealed. Abdullah remembered the massacre at Lod, and the cold efficiency of the Japanese who had sprayed the airport hall with bullets.

I would like to have seen that happen, he said, pursing his lips. They were brave men.

Yoshimitsu had stirred.

We are not with the Black September, he said simply. You know that. Our business here is our own. But it is the business of all men of honor to live on their own in power and simplicity. And the one we seek to kill is an obstacle to that. We have no grudge against him, or any man. We seek only to restore the independence and the honor of the old Japan.

I understand, said Abdullah as he poured more coffee. Our people have a light in common.

Upstairs, above the shop with its glittering silver and copper work, and the little private room where Abdullah had served the coffee, the two Japanese turned away from the moon and the sea. Reaching down to their waists, they began to unfasten the cords of their ceremonial swords, unslinging them from the broad belt of the obi. Beside them in the small bare anteroom they stood in were two long rows of beautifully worked lacquer sword racks, each one shaped to hold a pair of swords. Each bent in turn and reverently placed his weapon in its scabbard along the two curving holds of the rack, edge up and with the *ura* side to the wall.

Remember, Yamaka murmured, and he touched the silver *shishi* on the hilt.

Rising to his feet, he followed the old man through an

archway into the connecting room, walking with the long sweeping movement of an eighteenth-century samurai in court dress. Before him, Yoshimitsu progressed with the same movement, swinging the long trailing trousers of the court dress across the cool tiled floor. Together they reached the end of a long low wooden table, stretching the length of the room, and with a graceful movement, seated themselves on the ground in meditation.

This room was much larger than the other, vaulted with three domes, scooped out now into whitewashed hollows. Three high open windows gave views of the sea, and a cool breeze came in now from these. The distant sound of the waves was a quiet shush when the water stroked and withdrew from the shingle.

On the wall away from the sea, rich Persian rugs had been hung, and below them were smaller tables inlaid with marquetry and arched carving. The floor was tiled from wall to wall, and a coolness struck up from it through the ornate silks as the two Japanese knelt back on their heels.

I am ready, said Yoshimitsu.

At the other end of the room, behind their backs, was a second anteroom, the same size as the first. As Yoshimitsu spoke, Yamaka rose to his feet, and bowed. Then, with the same stately movement as before, he moved to the second anteroom and began to bring in a series of objects.

First of all, he carried in a small brazier of iron, in which a fire of charcoal was already blazing. Setting this down at Yoshimitsu's right side, he inspected the flame, blew on it, and knelt back for the old man to look.

It will do, he said.

Next, Yamaka returned with an iron kettle, filled with

water. This he placed on a grid across the fire, and left it to heat while he retired again to the anteroom. One after another, he brought in a lacquer box, a ceramic bowl, a long wooden spoon, and a small whisk. All these he laid carefully down before Yoshimitsu on the table. The old man inspected each in detail, and then curtly nodded.

Yamaka reseated himself at Yoshimitsu's right hand, and for a moment there was silence while the kettle came to a boil over the hot charcoal. The old man stared down at the traditional implements on the polished wood before him.

Let them come in, he said.

The forty-two men formed a magnificent and strange assembly as they wound up the stairs to the first anteroom, each dressed as Yamaka and Yoshimitsu had been, in the court dress of the eighteenth century. Hands came from long sleeves and rested on the twined hilts of their swords, feet sluffed in the long trousers over the tiles, there was the scent of strange perfume and incense. All wore their hair cut and bound in the traditional topknot, some with court caps, all with their clothes embroidered with the *mon* of the wild ginger plant.

As they milled and turned in the little room, bending to unfasten their swords and place them on the golden or black racks, they suggested all the glamour and finery of a clan gathering in Scotland or a primitive tribe assembly in New Guinea. But underneath the spectacle and the dazzle, there was the cold believing ardor of men indulging in a new religious ritual.

Yamaka came to the door to invite them in. Each bowed in turn and followed him in a prescribed and clearly understood order towards the long table where Yoshimitsu knelt for the ceremony. One after another, they entered and took their places down the length of the table on each side.

As they settled, each bowed again to the old man and then turned his eyes down in quiet meditation. No sound broke the silence save the swish of silks, the light soughing of the cool breeze, and the remote hissing of the sea.

When the last man had entered and settled, Yoshimitsu reached out and broke the seal on a long cardboard box to his left. Unfolding a set of Japanese papers, he laid open a selection of little green and brown sweet cakes, arranged in neat rows, and lightly covered with a sort of floury sugar. He extended the box to the man on his immediate left.

Please try one, he said with a smile.

While the man chose, and nibbled the cake, there was a sudden break in the tension and a light pleasant buzz of conversation around the table. The man smiled at Yoshimitsu.

Excellent, he said. We must give him our regular contract.

Yoshimitsu inclined his head and began to busy himself with the next operation. Taking off the lid of the lacquer caddy, he carefully measured out two portions of a dry green powder into the bowl, using the slender bamboo spoon to do so. Next, he took the kettle from the brazier and poured a quantity of boiling water over the powder, watching as it frothed and bubbled in the bowl. With the bamboo whisk, he swiftly beat and frothed the powder in the water into a thin green paste, about the consistency and color of pea soup, or spinach water. Then he turned the bowl and passed it to the man who had eaten the cake.

The conversation had died away again while the tea was made, and now there was a sort of expectant hush as the first guest drank. He smiled with pleasure, and congratulated Yoshimitsu. Again, general conversation broke out.

While the bowl went around the table, and was admired and praised as the tea itself had been, Yamaka watched from the old man's right hand, assisting with fresh water, or some comment on the consistency of the tea whenever one was required.

This is our last tea together, he thought, watching the impassive or animated faces of the friends he had come to know and work with for so long. Tomorrow, we shall be either more or less. There is no middle way. The night of the ronin will be over.

He began to picture the huge shape of the jet descending at the airport, its wings forming the shadow of the cross as it came in to land over Calvary. He saw the door open in the fuselage, the neat black-coated figure of the Prime Minister at the head of the ramp.

With an effort, he forced these images away. This was the moment of detachment before the action. It would do no good to anticipate the violence of the event. His thoughts veered, and he tried to hold them.

Let them survive, he said to himself. O let them all survive.

In the anteroom, the great swords lay on their racks and waited. They were never allowed inside a teahouse. It was their cross and their custom to lie in readiness in the bitter world outside. The blades slept in their scabbards, free of rust and free of responsibility. Theirs was the moment of action, direct as the stooping hawk in the long swing of resolution.

Inside the teahouse the Saviour of the Old Japan was serving his disciples with the traditional courtesy and humbleness. The human frame was less pure than the tempered body of a blade. It needed distraction and preparation. Before it could kill, it had to be cosseted and made ready.

The blades were ready now. They creaked a little in the soft magnolia wood. It had been a long time. Now that their exile was ending, they shivered a little in the salt air. They would need to be cleaned and oiled again after tomorrow. But tonight, like good horses, they could sniff the battle. The moon would shine in a few hours on the flash of their *yakiba*.

For the first time in three hundred years, said the spirit of the blades in the darkness. For the first time in three hundred years. There will be a night of swords.

The Hour of the Rat
12:00 midnight

21

The room was heavy with the scent of sweat and excited human flesh. There was a sense of lull, an expectant quality of something new and liberating about to happen. From where they sat close together in the semidarkness at a corner table, Valerian and Cadbury watched the gathered flower of the new Israel. These confident girls, with the long arms and the poised, athletic carriage, these smiling men, with their clear, watchful eyes and quick hands, these were the fruits of the cactus, the desert children who had won so many arid victories.

They look so healthy, said Valerian as he clonked the ice melting in his vodka-and-orange.

Even at midnight, said Cadbury.

Even at the hour of the rat.

They were quiet together, subdued already to their coming purpose, more submissive and absorptive than usual. Since their arrival at Lod Airport in the small hours of the morning, neither had slept. Events had moved with a ritual speed. The Israeli army had played its part with a cool and bitter efficiency Valerian had admired and been frightened by. In an hour's time the Trident carrying the Japanese Prime Minister on the first leg of his state visit would whistle down to land on the leveled runway only a mile away, and the equipment for what Valerian and Cadbury had come to do was already in position.

Valerian shifted on the bench. The cool of the glass between his fingers began to burn. He felt tense with a strange anxiety.

Poor buggers, he said.

Look, said Cadbury, leaning over and laying her hand on his arm, they tried to send me mad with an electric vibrator. They'd chop us both into diced carrots as soon as spit. I've killed two already. The rest are yours.

And you want them as much as Loyola does.

Valerian shuddered, remembering those gross pressures on his buttocks. Whatever happened, there was no going back.

Cadbury, he said. Supposing they don't come.

A tall, lithe girl in the uniform of an officer in the Israeli army went by with a glass in her hand. She smiled confidently down at Valerian as she passed.

They're Japanese, said Cadbury simply. They always come.

Valerian, she continued a minute later, watching his indrawn silence, it's a nasty and bloody business. But it has to be done. So get it together.

Valerian was far away. While the band was resting in this hot and cramped Israeli discotheque, with all the fears and doubts of his terrible vocation rising to the surface, he remembered his first race in the quarter-mile at school after his illness. For six years he had waited and recuperated, always being told by the doctors he would one day be able to run again.

I think you could, he recalled the old Scottish doctor saying as he wrapped his stethoscope in the basement room at Winslow Road. But don't overdo it.

So he had gone out into the sun, breathing real air for the first time, it seemed.

I can run again, he had said.

He had trained. Three times around the close each morning, like a slow rabbit. His ungrown lungs rasping and thick with the pain, his unused huge heart pounding like a steam engine.

At the sports day, he had entered for only two things, the two-twenty yards and the quarter-mile. He had won both easily in the days of his glory before the fever. It would come again, and he shivered with anticipation at the thought.

On their marks on the dry slightly windy spring day, six runners in the first heat had tensed and waited for the gun. It came and they were off, Valerian and a boy called Short well in the lead.

Valerian remembered his neck when the boy went ahead. The close blond hair, the high set of his muscles. And the force of his energy as his body began to pull him away in front.

I have to win, he remembered thinking. I have to win.

And then the enormous earth-shaking explosion of the pounding blood all through his body when he tried to sprint. The sudden cold realization that he was close to the limit of his effort. The bitter knowledge that the other boy was to beat him.

Shame flooded in Valerian still as he remembered his fall, lying face down panting for breath in the grass. Knowing he had given way to his fear and bitterness.

I've twisted my ankle, he had gasped when they ran up to ask what the matter was.

It was weeks later when another boy had forced him to face up to his real failure.

Perhaps you did, he had said with a grin. But it looked to me as if you just couldn't run another yard.

Valerian drained the last of the vodka. There would be no twisted ankles here in Israel. For Loyola, excuses were meaningless. And Valerian had no illusions about the sort of retribution he could bring to bear.

But screw your courage to the sticking place, said Cadbury, breaking in on his thoughts. Her hands ran over his belly under the table, and played for a second with their accustomed skill around the soft outlines of his pubis.

Valerian felt the stir of pleasure. He smiled, and kissed her on the forehead.

I need another drink, he said briskly.

As the waitress came by, he ordered another two vodka-and-oranges. He watched the receding sway of her hips with relaxed enjoyment while the lights went down for the end of the interval.

A cool blue spot began to play on the tight little stage at the end of the room and a sudden hush fell. A curtain parted, and four young men were there on the wood in a huge surge of applause. One lifted his hand, and a microphone on a stand was handed up from the floor. One settled himself at a bank of drums. The others stepped forward to flank the singer with their electric guitars. All four were naked to the waist, already sweating slightly. Long hair brushed their supple shoulders, metal jewelry gleamed at their necks and wrists, thick leather belts held in their crutch-tight silver lamé jeans.

When the shattering noise of the beat emerged in a sudden full-grown blaze from the banks of loudspeakers, the whole room focused and bloomed into concentrated attention. Drinks were forgotten, friends and conversations neglected. All eyes and ears fixed on the swaying sinuous line of the lead singer as his brown jeweled hands began to rotate the microphone stand in his fingers.

Unintelligible sexual words blossomed from his lips, un-ambiguous expressions of ecstatic, provocative joy distorted his features. His body moved, and the bodies of the others moved in time. It was group homosexual intercourse, and as fascinating to watch as a blue movie.

As Valerian watched, he felt a tingling of release in him. The job he would have to do in an hour's time seemed less demanding, less traumatic than before. He eased himself in his crisp off-white trousers, and allowed his eye to stray and fasten on the Israeli officer.

She was sitting with her legs crossed, her short military skirt laying bare a broad swathe of sun-tanned thighs. Her hand toyed with a glass. She was alone.

Sensing Valerian's gaze, her eye flitted over, rested on Cadbury, flitted away, then returned. In the harsh beat of the music, she stared straight into Valerian's eyes.

Let's have her over, Cadbury, he said, without shifting his gaze.

The girl looked up with an insolent smile when Cadbury

approached her. She liked the look of the Englishman's piece.

Cadbury paused above her, swaying her body from the hips to the beat of the rock. The half-naked men on the stage were gleaming with sweat, and their bodies moved increasingly to the active rhythms of awakening sexuality.

Cadbury bent and took the girl's neck in her hands. She leaned forward, pressing her belly into the soft female shoulders, massaging the tendons of the neck muscles.

Mmm, she said. You feel really beautiful. Come and meet my friend.

Rivolta, the girl said, with a sensuous grin. Speak English only a little. I like both. You, too, yes?

Oh, yes, said Cadbury softly, sliding the flats of her hands down over the girl's breasts in her tunic. Oh, yes. Oh, yes.

The drummer went into a frenzy, sticks flailing in a wild fantasy of jungle rhythms as the two girls came over to Valerian hand in hand. One on either side, they slid into place and pressed against him.

Rivolta, said Cadbury. This is Valerian. And I am Cadbury. From England.

The girl snuggled her head into Valerian's shoulder.

On the stage, the lead singer had begun to simulate the act of fornication with the microphone stand, hauling it close to his body and sliding his long, lithe legs down it. The hard jut of his penis forced his trousers into a fiercely erotic mound.

The audience had begun to respond. More and more couples were swaying to the beat; several had risen to their feet and were half dancing, half swaying to the stage.

We stand, please, said the Israeli girl. More feel of each other standing, yes.

On their feet in the hot sweet scent of human bodies, their arms interlaced in a sensuous trio. Behind him Valerian felt Cadbury run her fingers inside the waistband of his trousers, her belly rotating urgently against his buttocks. In front he could feel his organ hardening as the Israeli girl rubbed her bottom into him. His hands moved up and began to caress and knead her breasts through the tight military shirt.

The girl's head twisted around, and her tongue licked his lips.

Unfasten, please, she said softly, and her body revolved in excitement as Valerian's fingers undid the buttons of her shirt from behind. Underneath, a superb pair of breasts, the nipples erect and quivering with delight, swung loose into his palms.

There was something incredibly erotic in this public yet secret handling. All around, the shattering noise of the music was like a screen or curtain.

Behind him Valerian could feel Cadbury opening her blouse. Against his back, the heat of her body was greater, and he felt the pressure and rubbing of her naked breasts on his spine. Her fingers slid down over his belly, clasping and stroking his pubic hair.

I love the rock, said Rivolta, twisting her head again, her tongue flicking out and entering Valerian's mouth as he bent forward over her. At the same moment he felt Cadbury's quick hands on the zipper of his fly. There was an easing of the nylon over his penis, and his firm erection had been taken out and was being openly handled in her fingers.

On the stage, the singer had the microphone thrust between his legs. He bent down over it, extending his taut buttocks provocatively towards the lead guitarist. They began to rotate while the guitarist swung his instrument as if to caress and sodomize him.

All over the room, hands had begun to clap in time. Pairs of arms were up over heads clashing together in a solid mass of common involvement. Rivolta turned around and kissed Valerian full on the lips.

The music rose and climaxed. The lead singer seemed to soar up into a high squeal of pure delighted release. The guitarist took him around the waist, the bulge in his groin pressed hard, as if thrusting deep inside him against those bursting lamé trousers.

Please come. Please come now, gasped Rivolta, withdrawing her lips and tongue. And Valerian felt his sperm gush and spurt below the girl's skirt as she rolled back and ground her naked buttocks into his belly.

Later, as all three resettled in their corner seat, they felt a huge relaxation. Other couples and trios had perhaps been doing the same. No one seemed to have noticed. Disheveled as they were, they sat with their arms around each other's shoulders, breasts naked under open shirts, Valerian with his trousers still undone.

This is Israel, Rivolta said. Land of freedom. Here you must come again, yes.

But Valerian knew he would never come again. It came to him as he sat in this corner of the Dead Sea Discotheque that this was the last climax. He felt a strange acceptance. He was ready now for whatever had to be done.

I knew a man once, he said, as Cadbury had said to Alexis, who believed you had only so many orgasms. When you'd used up your ration, that was it. The trouble was, you never knew when the time was up.

For Israel, Rivolta said seriously, the time is always up.

Cadbury said nothing. She watched the hands on the watch of a man at the next table. They stood together at the top of the dial. It was midnight, the hour of the rat.

22

As the Trident began to lose altitude, the Prime Minister looked out through the ovoid plexiglass of the window at the remote lights and glitter of Tel Aviv. It spread below him to his right, like a long chain of costume jewelry, along the surf line of the eastern Mediterranean. He fingered the brandy glass at his elbow, allowing his thoughts to skate freely over the events of the next few hours.

Fasten your seat belts, please, said the voice of the stewardess over the intercom.

The Prime Minister did as he was asked. He had a strong sense of obedience, and an even stronger sense of modesty. Traveling with only the usual appurtenances of security and refinement had been part of his deliberate policy in the three years since his party had achieved its startling majority in the Diet, and he had shifted from being a mere ex-minister of economics to the virtual ruler and arbiter of the destiny of Japan.

I am only the edge of the people's voice, he had said deprecatingly, on more than one occasion, to foreign journalists. But the general view among Tokyo-watchers was that Ito Takada was the most powerful Japanese citizen since the Second World War.

I believe in the Emperor, he would say. I believe in the people. They are one voice, one entity. I am merely their passing servant.

But the Emperor had grown more and more involved in his marine biology, endlessly sifting and examining the varieties of sting ray in his private station off the coast of Kyushu. If Takada needed Imperial support, he knew how to get it. Most of the time, he didn't.

The note of the engines changed. The huge plane began to drift and fall, sweeping in a low slow arc over fields and houses, armies and people, all scattered and enveloped in the quiet heat and darkness. The Prime Minister sucked the last of the armagnac into his throat and swallowed. He was a Socialist, but he was also a gourmet.

He wiped his lips, and glanced out of the corner of his eye at his secretary dozing in the seat to his left. An ambitious, precise, underfed young man in his late twenties. He would never get where he wanted. On the other side of the aisle, the alert young geisha was watching as his head turned. She smiled and made a *moue* with her lips.

Move over, said the Prime Minister softly. I want to land with Onroku.

The secretary was instantly awake. He undid his seat belt and slid out into the aisle. The girl took his place and leaned over to put her head on the Prime Minister's shoulder. Then her long fingers began to knead and mold the tense muscles in his arms and back.

Is that better, Minnaloushe? she said very gently.

The Prime Minister ignored her, as she had learned to know he would. He needed the attention of love to focus his concentration. He was already at the crowded desk in his head, shifting the minutiae of the future to a fresh alignment.

She allowed her fingers to stray over his neck, then return to their firm pressure and reassurance.

The Prime Minister watched the dark masses of the ground rise up and flicker past. His mind ran with the plane's shadow over the warning he had had by the violet scrambler only four hours ago.

Xetox 4, it had said, the package is waiting for you at the airport.

Have arrangements made, he had replied. But allow the English to cope.

He reflected now on the likelihood of his guess being

right. Only he of the thirteen people on board the Trident knew that an attempt would shortly be made on his life. He was a brave and philosophical man. A lifetime in the practice of Zen had taught him that every man had his own time. If tonight was the time for Ito Takada, so be it. He was ready.

As the wheels came down to kiss the ground, and the huge reversal of the jets began, he wondered if perhaps his decision had been the correct one.

Nothing, he thought to himself, but nothing, must be allowed to interfere with my talks in Jerusalem. If the Israelis begin to suspect that I am here to exploit our reputation for violence, we are lost. There must be no government thugs to protect me. No official guns. No bitter memories of the little yellow men in Burma. The conspiracy will kill itself by its failure to kill me. And the Israelis will see me as a man of peace.

The great airplane began to slow, grinding to a halt on the tarmac. All around there was the unclicking of seat belts, the sense of relaxation of a safe arrival. The Prime Minister shivered slightly, and the girl looked at him with concern.

I love you, Onroku, he said with a smile.

Be careful, Minnaloushe, she said seriously. I know there is danger.

He patted her hand as they stood up together.

The windows were all wound down in the old bus parked on the boundary of the airport. The forty-four men in the cramped interior sat staring out across the tarmac towards the black growing shape of the landing Trident in the distance. It was hot, and they sweated while they waited.

Light from the moon filtered in on their impassive faces, over the woven silk of their kimonos, the triple leaves of the wild ginger plant revealed or broken in the fall and flow of the silk, the faint glow catching on knuckles tight over sword hilts, or on the backs of the hard seats.

The hour of the rat, said Yoshimitsu. The poison is there in the bird's belly.

The sound of the Trident's engines carried over the field as a dull roar, almost a protest or a call to battle. The great plane began to taxi closer, as if challenging them to come out and fight.

Two minutes, said the driver of the bus.

Flat out, said Yoshimitsu. And leave the rest to us.

The samurai eased their swords in the darkness. The long blades quivered in the scabbards. The moment of blood was here.

Two hundred yards away, on the back of an open truck, Valerian watched the Trident with his hands on the double grips of the Lewis gun. At his side he could feel Cadbury's hair on his cheek, the warmth of her body against his thigh. The long, greasy belts of the ammunition lay in her hands, the first already fed into the chambers.

Behind them, half a battalion of Israeli troops was in cover behind the airport buildings. But Loyola had had his way. The Service had begun it, and the Service was to be allowed to complete the job. Valerian would initiate the attack, and he would get support only in the last emergency.

The Jew-boys really prefer it that way, Loyola had said to Valerian on the scrambler. The man with the black patch has had his fill of being regarded as a sort of trigger-happy sand-boy. So it's do it yourself for you, Valerian, dear. And don't let the jumping bullets give you a premature ejaculation. We may have other uses for you.

Valerian lay now in the sour stink of the truck, his bush shirt open at the neck, a sunburned patch smarting a little from overexposure to the raw light. He felt very calm, and he knew there would be no need of support from the Israelis. When he pressed the grips of the Lewis gun there would be one man in the sights before him, a short squat man, with a boar's mask over his face, who had broken his pride at London airport. And there would be no question of missing.

Two minutes, love, said Cadbury in the darkness.

As the Prime Minister came to the door of the plane, he wondered when they would make their attempt. He paused at the top of the flight of the steps. He suspected not yet. More probably when he was on the ground.

He looked down at the assembled group of people. The Israeli dignitaries in their neat summer suits. The airport personnel with tools and cans of oil. There was a cool breeze, and he realized that his face was wet with sweat when it touched him. He began to descend the steps, followed by his secretary and the girl.

No band, he thought. No music.

It felt very still, and the time seemed to pass slowly while his feet moved on the rubber over the aluminum. He forced his features into a smile, and lifted his left hand in greeting.

From the shadow of the plane he stepped out and onto

the soil of Israel. A small man with a neat black mustache came forward and shook his hand.

Welcome to Tel Aviv, he said.

They began to walk side by side away from the Trident towards the airport buildings. Around them, a small group fell into step. The Prime Minister was not listening to the rapid social conversation flowing around him. The muscles in his neck were tense with expectation.

Since you asked us to, the small neat man was saying, we avoided a military escort.

The Prime Minister smiled. They were eighty yards or more from the shelter of the airport buildings. In the dazzling glare of arc lights they walked slowly forward.

At the wheel of the bus, Yamaka had his eye fixed on the watch at his wrist. When the Prime Minister and his escort were twenty paces from the Trident, he spoke.

Now, he said.

In the name of the new shogunate, said Yoshimitsu, rising to his feet. Rise and kill him.

As his bare feet hit the tarmac, Yamaka felt all his past shrink into a tiny ball of clay and roll away to one side. His voice rose in his throat and burst in spite of himself out of his lips.

Ieyasu, he found himself crying. Ieyasu.

One after another the samurai began to debouch from the bus, blades naked in their hands, the light silk of the kimonos no impediment to their free movement in the warm night air.

They were running. In a tight group, one solid body of

will and muscle, like the first wave of the bombers that wiped out Pearl Harbor, they moved across bare tarmac towards the little civilian group between the airplane and the buildings.

It was the hour of the rat.

Move, screamed Valerian. They're coming.

The barrel of the Lewis gun swung on its axis under his hands as the driver swung the truck in a wide arc across the tarmac to allow him a free field of fire.

Through the cross hair of the sights, he squinted down at the steady body of running men. They seemed incredibly small and distant, as remote from his present purposes as ants on the moon.

For Christ's sake, start to fire, said Cadbury.

His fingers squeezed on the grips. He felt the gun kick and the long belts chatter through the gates as Cadbury fed them in. There was the bitter smell of burning, the grips slippery with his sweat. A line from a long-forgotten poem came suddenly into his mind.

The Gatling's jammed, he muttered to himself. The Gatling's jammed.

No, it fucking hasn't, he heard Cadbury saying. Just kill the bleeders with it. Kill the fucking lot of them.

As the bullets tore out across the tarmac, the truck raced to a new position. The samurai had begun to fall when the gun started. Valerian watched them go down one after another, as in a slow-motion film.

The Prime Minister flung himself flat and rolled violently

to one side. His entourage began to shout and dodge. With one eye, he could see the remote phalanx of running men, hear the terrible shout of "Ieyasu" as they began to close in, watch them fall and kick as the bullets began to bring them down.

My poor people, he said aloud. My poor people.

To the samurai, running in their own dream, it was never possible that their act could fail. Each one felt sure the others would come through. Some blood would have to be shed to give the cause its future glory.

Blades in their hands, they died running. As each fell, the blade flew or dropped from his hands in a silver cascade of metal across the tarmac, floodlit by the moon and the arc lights. Flesh and iron lay side by side in their shattered pride.

To Yamaka, as he fell, it seemed he had been smitten by the divine wind that would save Japan once again from the foreign corruption. As the bullets tore into his chest, he staggered in a strange blaze of lights. Focusing his eyes on the little group around the Prime Minister, he swung the long *katana* in his hand and let it fly through the air in the direction of his own run.

Follow the blade, he cried, and his body pitched down in his blood.

Only Yoshimitsu knew, when he heard the sound of the Lewis gun, that he had been betrayed.

Betrayed, he said as he ran. Betrayed. The English and their master Loyola were too clever for me.

But he knew that it made no difference. As he felt the rough tarmac under the hard soles of his running feet, he was again back with his ancestors in the Kamakura period, a free samurai in the days of the wars.

Die well, he said to himself. Die well, and save those you can.

And then the bullets started to hit him.

Yoshimitsu crawled forward. Each foot was a terrible journey over miles of rock and scrub. He paused for breath, staunching the flow of blood from his leg with his hand. The long thin blade dragged on the tarmac beside him.

Intermittently, he was back in Kyoto as a child, playing hide-and-seek with his friends. But the vision would slip, and his sense of purpose would return. He knew where he was going.

Silence the gun, he said to himself. I must silence the gun.

Now as he dragged himself towards the truck from behind, he heard the gun stop firing. There was a dead lull, then the high squeal of whistles, and the sound of men in boots running.

I have failed, he said to his shadow as he crawled. They are all dead.

He reached the back of the truck with a last burst of energy. There was no sign of the man firing.

Very quietly he hauled himself up.

Valerian lay slumped forward over the gun. He felt exhausted. A huge bitterness was seeping through him.

The poor buggers, he said. They never had a chance.

As he lifted himself to wipe the oil from his forehead, the old Japanese made his final effort. There was a slight sound when his foot caught on the side of the truck.

Look out, Valerian, cried Cadbury as she spun around and saw the raised blade.

But it was too late. Her hand came out and deflected Yoshimitsu's arm as the blade came down. And Valerian felt his world explode into pain and darkness as the razor edge turned in to achieve its revenge.

My Christ, said Cadbury, on her knees. Valerian. Don't die. Oh, please, don't die.

The Prime Minister walked among the bodies. Sometimes he turned one over with his foot, looking down at a face he knew or was struck by. Beside him the ambulances waited, with their blue lights spinning, the Israeli drivers handling their stretchers and equipment.

There isn't much to carry away, said the secretary.

The Prime Minister pursed his lips.

They wanted a new Japan, he said. But they wanted it with the old methods.

He turned on his heel and began to walk towards the airport buildings. The girl came forward and took his arm. The world began to rebuild itself in its familiar, safe form.

Yoshimitsu is dead, said the girl. There will be no revolution.

The Prime Minister looked up at the stars. They seemed to lie on the black asphalt of the sky like the broken swords of the samurai.

It will come again, he said. For us, it will always come again.

THE HOUR OF THE OX

2:00 A.M.

23

Valerian lay in the back of the truck. He was aware of a kind of total stickiness. His chest and legs seemed to be thickly coated with some viscous substance that made him feel itchy and hot, as if he needed a bath. He wondered vaguely what it was. It ought to be blood, or sweat perhaps, but he was sure it was more like a kind of treacle.

I'd like a wash, he heard himself saying. Would you help me to go to the bathroom?

He knew there was no point in having a wash, and he tried to laugh at his own silliness. It was funny laughter. It sounded to him much more like coughing. He felt a jerky, racking sensation.

I need a wash, he said. Oh, Christ, I need a wash.

This time it was his own voice, and he looked out through his own eyes up at the constellation of Orion directly above his head. He tried hard to focus on the exact center of the sword belt. It seemed to Valerian that if he could achieve this focus, he could halt the gradual spread of the stickiness through his body. There was something increasingly loathesome about it, and he began to shudder uncontrollably. He had the sense of a giant snail dragging its length slowly up from the ankles to the neck.

Orion, he said aloud. I think you have the most beautiful sword belt I've ever seen. Passing the girdles of women. I think the jewel in the center is the garnet of my own birthstone. It keeps me safe from any illness to have it around my neck. Did you know that? Are you a Capricorn, too?

Valerian began to hear his own words doubling and blurring. He was unsure if he was speaking aloud or to himself, and he felt very preoccupied about the propriety of talking in this way at all. He became lost in confusion about this, and he was a little happier because it distracted him from the sticky progress of the snail.

The night was very hot. The army doctor wiped sweat from under his armpits as he fitted the stethoscope into his ears and bent over Valerian's chest. The plain cloth of the shirt had been ripped back, and the light fur in the hollow of his ribs was exposed. To Cadbury, as she knelt beside him, he seemed unnaturally thin and brittle. It was as if the stroke of the sword had reduced him by some occult magic to an earlier and more vulnerable element of himself. She reached out and delicately touched the curling hair, soaked with sweat under her hand.

It's really a cup for your breasts, he had said once about this curious dip in his chest. I had it made specially. As you feel, my dear Cadbury, it's a perfect fit.

She had snuggled down, her body half over his, her left nipple erect in the bony cavity between his ribs.

I adore your cup, she had said. And now it's full of milk.

The doctor folded his stethoscope and leaned back on his heels. He looked sideways at Cadbury.

His heart is very weak, he said. I'll give him some more morphine for the pain.

He snapped open the leather case on the floor of the truck, lifting out a disposable syringe in its plastic sheath. He broke the cap on the morphine capsule, and dipped the needle in the tube. Cadbury watched while the liquid rose in the syringe against the background of the stars.

Here, said the doctor. Wipe this on his arm.

He gave Cadbury the bottle of alcohol and a swab of cotton wool, watching as she rolled back Valerian's sleeve and dabbed the anesthetic on his skin. Swiftly and efficiently, he bent and inserted the needle, pressing till the syringe was empty.

O.K., he said. Now wipe it again. And hold it on.

He placed the syringe in a cardboard bag as Cadbury dabbed the skin again and held the little swab of cotton wool tightly in place over the lesion.

He may talk soon, said the doctor gently. But he can't last more than half an hour.

Cadbury nodded. They had told her as soon as they reached the truck that there was no chance of moving Valerian. The little Israeli doctor had looked down at him while the ambulance stood by with its siren full on and the blue light spinning round and round in the darkness.

No chance, he had said. No chance at all.

The stroke of the sword had gone in just above the groin, thrusting up into several outlets when the blade turned. It was like the fingers of a hand, the doctor had said. The weapon seemed to reach in and feel for the vital parts.

Just the same as the horn of a bull, he had said. It's the

multiple-entry places. If we try to move him, he'll die in minutes. Left here, he might have an hour.

So Valerian was dying, as he might have wished, with his boots on, in the back of a truck beside his machine gun, with the sword of Yasutsuna, which had killed him, naked behind his head, like a loving woman after her climax.

Resting her eyes on the sword, Cadbury reflected on all that it had cost. The body of Yamaka face down on the tarmac, riddled with bullets. The body of Yoshimitsu, dead a few yards away. The body of Valerian, dying.

Valerian, she murmured softly. My poor Valerian. What was the point of it all?

But she knew the answer. For all those in the Service, the blood and pain were their own explanation. The dream of sex was the dream of violence, and they had only this to live by until they died. The surfaces of the missions were only surfaces, the structures of the operations were only myths. They were blunt instruments, and they died when they grew too sharp.

She shook herself, and withdrew her gaze from the glinting steel. That way lay madness and self-deceit. She still had a job to do.

Valerian, she said, stroking his hair. Valerian. Can you hear me, lover?

Valerian heard the strange voices in the darkness. The stickiness had become a kind of transferred echoing, as if viscosity had been bartered for blurred noise. He had a curious sense of wading. He was knee-deep, then thigh-deep, in a sewer of moving sounds. He felt disembodied, as if left with only one sense, the sense of hearing, out of which he had to construct the whole world of what was happening. It seemed to be a journey through a long low tunnel towards a tight small room where everything was more intense, more concentrated.

Are you there, said a voice. Are you coming yet.

Valerian felt his world of sound shift into one of sudden trembling pressures, a kinesthetic world where everything took place as a touch on his skin. Tiny insects crawled or jumped or swam all over him, and he felt aware of a total involvement in a huge process of minuscule change and excitation, as if he was the turning globe with all its animal and vegetable life in constant flux.

I feel so privileged, he said.

Once again he began to worry about whether he should have said this, or indeed whether he had said it at all. A sense of dissolving began to overcome him, and he allowed himself to sink with it. He was going down, as if in a fast elevator.

First floor. Ladies lingerie, he heard himself saying, and then the insane cackling of what might be his own laughter.

He's coming round, said the doctor, with his hand on Valerian's pulse. I think he'll die conscious. But it won't be long.

He got to his feet and climbed down over the side of the truck to the tarmac. Lighting a cigarette, he walked a few yards away and left them together.

Cadbury stretched the muscles of her cheeks. She felt worn and tired. The hair seemed to straggle into her eyes, and she shook it loose. She must somehow keep awake. She eased her position and gently massaged the muscles of Valerian's shoulders.

Overhead an Israeli fighter went by with a shattering flare of noise, red light winking from its nose and tail. A breath of cool air came, and she sucked it in gratefully.

Valerian remembered the Royal Hospital. He was twelve years old, flat on his back in the second week after his rheumatic fever had started. Screens were around three other beds in the ward, and at night he heard the groans of the men dying. He watched them sliding an old man into the long yellow body of an iron lung. It lay on the other side of the ward, squared off and terrible like a crashed bomber with its wings ripped off.

Mummy, he said, when will I come home.

But she hadn't known, and the doctors had told him nothing. Except that he wouldn't be able to play games again for a bit. He thought of the little Czech doctor sitting on the edge of the iron bed, with his serious face and his bad news.

No football? he had asked incredulously. No running?

They had given him books, sandwiches for tea, doses of that filthy medicine twice a day. And the endless aspirins that had ruined his heart. He remembered the cold feel of the metal slabs on his wrists and ankles as the electro-cardiograph checked the motions of his blood.

Ten weeks it had taken, and his mind broken forever, he thought, by the fear and depression of loneliness and inactivity. But at last he had walked again. And had come home to the little semidetached house with the marble statue in the garden, and the old woman next door dying of angina.

Valerian felt the elevator rising. He was thirteen, he was having his first recurrence, he was writing his film script for the school film society. The elevator was rising faster. He could feel his heart starting to beat, the heavy thunderous drumming of life and pain. The dull remote ache in his side grew closer and became a sharp gnawing. Valerian felt the elevator break through the roof. His eyes opened.

Hello, Cadbury, said Valerian.

Hello, love.

Valerian looked into her gray eyes, full of a strange close love he could do nothing now to sustain or cherish. He lifted his left hand and gently pushed the yellow hair back from her cheeks. He felt the moisture of tears on them.

Don't cry, he said. This is how I always wanted it.

She shook her head.

Don't cry, he said. Let me do the talking. There are three last things I have to say. And there isn't long.

He felt the edge of the pain scrape along the bone of his pelvis, creeping like the teeth of a shark up into his softer parts. He closed his eyes, blinked, and opened them again, like a man surfacing from a deep dive.

It was Loyola, he said. He was hand in glove with the samurai from the start. And then he betrayed them. He knew the truth all the time. But he wanted you tested. He wanted us both tested. He knew I was weak, and he was right.

He felt the drumming increase in volume inside his body,

and the rhythm change. It was heavier, and more irregular now. The pain had halted, as if to get its second wind. On the other side of a small valley, he could see the orgasm of his own death approaching.

The second thing, he said, and then he was coughing.

Cadbury held his shoulders, and stroked his brow with her hand. It was burning hot.

The second thing, he said. I broke the rules. I was never detached enough. I always wanted you for yourself as well as for your body. I needed props.

Valerian felt his power to speak slowly drifting away. The drumming had grown until it filled his ears and his interest. He had to concentrate on it; there was a special message for him in it. There was no time left for Cadbury. With a huge effort, he pulled himself back.

Valerian sat upright in the truck. Reaching out, he caught Cadbury by the shoulders and pressed his lips on hers. His left hand felt for the zipper of his trousers, fumbled, dragged it down. His right hand felt for hers, pulled it to him, pressed it in through the cloth, parting the nylon of his pants so that it lay on the calmed machine of his penis.

Break the mirrors, Cadbury, he said. Break all the mirrors.

Valerian fell back, and his eyes glazed.

In Valerian's dream, they carried his body very gently down to the shore and laid it along the sweetly scented planks of cedar in the boat. He smelled the resin of the torches when they dipped them before lighting. All around he listened to the chink of metal and the shuffle of sandals as the warriors gathered for his funeral. His fixed eyes looked up at the star belt of Orion in the northern sky, and then into the gray eyes of the helmeted faces bending over him to pay their last respects, grief and pride mingled under the flaxen hair and the clear skin.

Then he felt the warmth around his ankles and at his neck as the dry brushwood was lit. He heard the flames crackle, and the sound of the women's lamentation begin, the thin high wailing of the Viking death chant. The waves lapped at the keel, and he heard the scrunch and splash of thonged legs in water as they waded in to push the boat away from its moorings.

Overhead, the moon shone down on the water, and the boat gathered way as the wind caught the sails. Now the flames leaped higher, and he felt the burning lick at his clothes and his skin. His lips drew back in a smile, and he saw the clouds break over the stars, unveiling the ranked warriors on the plains of Valhalla, their swords crossed on their shields while they waited.

Cadbury sat for a long time without moving. Then she withdrew her hands from Valerian's body and got to her feet. She picked up the sword from behind his head and climbed over the side of the truck to the ground. The scabbard lay beside the body of Yoshimitsu, and she bent to pick it up. A few yards away, the army doctor was standing smoking.

He's dead, said Cadbury. But you'd better check.

She turned and walked away across the tarmac towards the airport perimeter. The cool wind blew, and she felt it ruffle her hair. After she had gone about fifty yards, she stopped. Looking up at the sky, she searched for Orion. Then she looked down at the gleaming blade of the sword, and with a single quick movement rammed it back forever into its sheath.

Good-bye, Valerian, she said.

24

As the Ferrari came up from the circle onto the M4, Cadbury reached out her left hand to start the wipers. It had begun to snow, and the big soft flakes were swirling in ever denser clouds into her field of vision. The car heater was broken, and she shivered a little in her light dress, moving her hand again to run up the off-side window, through which the chill air was seeping, thick with melting crystals. The quiet electric hiss was soothing, and she felt warmer already as she swung out into the middle lane.

It was three o'clock, and there were no other cars on

the road. The straight blaze of the headlights extended
and broadened when Cadbury pulled the switch out to
full beam. The tiny blue light glared at her from the
dashboard. She eased herself on the cold cream leather,
gently revolving her shoulders and tensing the muscles
above her knees.

Christ, I'd like a massage, she thought.

She felt a hard pang in her belly as she remembered the
last massage she had had, and Valerian's long expert hands
swooping and kneading her trapezoids. She had been very
tired, and, for her, unusually bored with the idea of sex.

We'll have a massage instead, Valerian had said.

Massage?

Lie down on your belly. I'll show you.

She had turned on the mattress and felt Valerian draw
back the sheets and then ease the long dress up over her
buttocks and tuck it under her shoulders. He had dropped
his trousers and knelt over her closed legs in his tight
pants, the firm rod of his penis already erect when it
brushed the cleft of her bottom.

Valerian, she had said.

It's just a massage. Just a massage. Now lie still.

She had closed her eyes and turned her face down into
the pillow, breathing in the warmth of the sheets as his
hands began to press and slap at her back.

Now as the car snarled into third gear, and she flung it
across towards the fast lane in the gathering avalanche
of white swirling snow, Cadbury remembered the violence
and the gentle tenderness of Valerian's hands. The shock
of the pain when he dug his fingers into the knots of tension in her neck and brows. The cool delicious luxury of

the oil as it poured and flowed into the crevice of her spine. The tingling and diffused sexual joy while he pummeled and slapped the loose flesh of her buttocks with the flats of his palms.

The wipers cleared their arcs of glass into the shapes of Japanese fans, now moving faster as Cadbury switched them to their second speed. The windshield was coated with a wide layer of blanketing white as the car rammed forward at seventy, at eighty, into the darkness.

Cadbury blinked. She needed all her concentration to keep the car on a level course through the snow. Valerian was dead, and she would never feel his hands on her body again.

She drove faster, as if in a cocoon of glass, a winter snowstorm toy that someone had turned upside down on a dressing table. There was nothing else in the world. Only her and the car. And Valerian lying in his grave beside the sea in Israel.

She had stood there yesterday in the brilliant sun, sweating a little in an army shirt, as they lowered the coffin into the broken ground. There had been a short anonymous service, a prayer and a hymn. No one had known Valerian's religious views, and in Tel Aviv death was cheap. They had wanted him buried quickly, and Cadbury had been too locked up to care.

Of course, we could ship his body home, the little Colonel had said in his hot office, fanning himself with a copy of *Mayfair*. But I think it's best if we keep the whole affair under wraps. I gather that your masters would prefer a quiet funeral.

And a plot in the Protestant cemetery.

Of course, he had said. Very easy to arrange.

So Valerian had been hurried into the earth beside the expatriate English he had had so little in common with. The soil had rattled down on the polished walnut of his last box, and Cadbury had tossed some imported iris and daffodils into the grave. She remembered that that was what he had done for his mother, and it seemed appropriate.

No one else had come to the grave, and Cadbury had stood there alone for a time. While the sun burned down, and the long line of the surge broke on the shore in the distance, she had spoken aloud to Valerian.

You were my master for two years, she had said. I don't say I loved you, because I doubt if I ever loved anybody except my father. But you were the center of what I did, and what I believed in. You taught me to work for the Service. You made me think it mattered. And when it stopped mattering for you, it had made me strong enough to keep you going. For long enough to complete this job. And to kill you.

Cadbury had knelt by the grave and stroked the soil gently with her fingers. A slight breeze had come, disheveling her hair.

Forgive me, Valerian, she had said. I have to go back. And I have to keep on working for them. I haven't anything else now. With you, I might have abandoned it, if we'd come through, and you'd wanted it. But not now. I have to go back. But I won't forget you. Not ever.

The needle of the speedometer wavered at one hundred

on its black ground, and the car bored forward down its long tunnel of snow-thronged light. A small van flashed back in the middle lane, and Cadbury fixed her eyes again through the wipers after a brief glance at it in the rear-view mirror. Even if it was the police, they would scarcely bother to try racing a Ferrari in this weather.

For a moment she considered letting go of the wheel. To be killed in the Ferrari, in a snowstorm, three weeks away from Christmas. The needle had drifted up to a hundred and twenty, and the car had developed its most beautiful high-pitched scream. In spite of herself, she found that she was concentrating on the road.

It would make the paperwork too easy, she thought. I can just see Loyola's face.

But she tried to resist that particular image. As her hands adjusted their grip on the wheel, she remembered the radio, and her hand reached out to switch it on. It was the original radio for the car, and its performance was erratic. By some miracle, tonight it was in excellent form. A French singer came over her shoulder from the loudspeaker below the back window. Through the mildest crackling, the words drifted around and soothed her thoughts.

Poor car, she said aloud. You're no more a coffin than a cradle. We have to go on as adults.

Her foot slackened on the accelerator, and the big car growled as it slowed. Cadbury began to think of her flat, the central heating already on, food in the refrigerator, her letters brought in and laid out by the madame from the brothel whom she had cabled yesterday about her return. And Alexis. Alexis awake and eager to see her.

In a sudden rush of affection and desire, she remembered the long curve of the borzoi's body, the hot licking of his tongue, the heavy panting when he rose to greet her.

Alexis, she murmured as she drove. My poor boy. You must have missed me so much.

Alexis.

The word echoed through the empty house in the darkness. Cadbury had had the dog running in her mind all the way off the M4 and down the North Circular and into London. Parking the long blue car in the mews, she had imagined the rough power of his body along hers, the enormous joy of his need for her and his delight at her return.

In the icy snow, fumbling to unfasten the trunk and dig her suitcase out, she had blinked and seen his image. It had seemed to sum up the pleasures of returning home, all the comfort and domesticity the Service so often denied her and that she suddenly felt she so urgently needed. She had left the trunk open and run up the narrow flight of stairs, almost tripping over the milk bottles and a small parcel that had been left for her at the top.

Feeling for her key, she had run her eye over the soaked brown paper. It was a London postmark, and a handwriting she didn't immediately recognize. Opening the door, she had slid her suitcase in and lifted the parcel in her hands. It was quite light, she noticed as she called the dog's name.

Alexis.

———

She waited for him to come, eager for the feel of his exquisite shape before she switched on the light and saw him. It was strange that he needed to be called twice. He was usually aware of her arrival by some sixth sense before she had even opened the door. And then it occurred to her that perhaps the madame had taken him downstairs to look after and play with while she was away.

Relaxing, she switched on the light in the hall and walked through to the bedroom with the parcel in her hand. There seemed to be a slightly unfamiliar scent in the room, and Cadbury tried to identify it as she picked up a pair of scissors to cut the string on the parcel.

Rotten meat, she thought. That's it.

She walked through to the kitchen, toeing open the refrigerator to see what the madame had left unattended to turn bad and make a smell. But there seemed to be nothing there. She bent to sniff in the cold bright opening. There was milk and cheese, butter, bacon, a can or two of orange juice. All in good condition.

She stood up and looked about the room. Perhaps Alexis had left something half-eaten before he had been taken away. Or perhaps there was a dead mouse.

Cadbury paused, her hands white as her knuckles dug into the hard surface of the parcel. Unconsciously, she began to unravel the paper as she turned to go into the bathroom. Before she got there and switched on the light, she knew what she was going to find. But it made very little difference to the shock.

———

Alexis lay on the tiles behind the bath, his long body curiously rigid, as if built on a sort of metal frame. Blood had run from him over the tiles down the sides of the porcelain, and there were rivulets of dried red along the bottom, where a nest of spiders and flies had settled to feed. The smell was stronger here, and Cadbury found herself retching involuntarily when she stepped down into the bath and reached over to touch the dead dog's fur.

He rolled on his side under her hand, and his head flopped forward. Cadbury remembered the photographs of the preserved corpses from the bogs in Denmark, and how the expressions had seemed to vary between peacefulness and horror. She wondered what the expression meant on Alexis's face.

The middle of the dog's body was completely mutilated. It took a moment for Cadbury to realize what had been done to him, and then she vomited into the bath.

Later, back in the bedroom, she opened the parcel. The brown paper concealed the long elegant shape of a *fubako*, a Japanese box for conveying letters or messages. The box was elegantly fastened with a silk tasseled cord, and the lacquered surface showed the moon above a riot of moving clouds. It was picked out in silver from the gold *nashiji* ground.

Cadbury slowly lifted the lid, and looked down at the carefully folded white tissue, with the little note on top of it. She laid aside the note and unfolded the tissue.

There was very little blood. Just the delicate pink flesh and the silky fur of the dog's penis, neatly and efficiently severed at the root by some sharp cutting instrument. It lay like a strange exotic fruit in the box, a present or a warning for some personage of great importance.

Cadbury looked at it for a long time before she laid it aside and picked up the note. It contained a simple message. *Detach yourself. Loyola.*

The flat seemed very quiet. Cadbury went through to the bedroom and stood in front of her long wall mirror. Slowly she unbuttoned her long blouse and slipped out of the sleeves. She unzipped her skirt and let it fall to her feet. Rolling down the blue tights to her ankles, she stepped out of her skirt and her shoes, and pulled the tights over her toes. She tucked her hand into the tiny slip of her black panties and drew them down over her thighs and calves until she could step out of these, too.

Naked, she stood and looked at herself in the mirror. The long yellow hair hung down in soft silky folds onto her shoulders. The gray eyes were clear and untired. The warm full lips were a little compressed, but still curving and beautiful. She ran her hands over the taut warm skin of her breasts, feeling the brown aureoles around her nipples, and letting her fingers sweep in and down over her navel to her belly. She stroked the thick mat of golden fur in her groin, turned on one side and looked over her shoulder at the swell of her buttocks.

I belong to the Service, she said.

In bed, under the white goat's fur, Cadbury lay on her belly with her legs wide apart. It was a long time before sleep came. Outside, the snow settled gently over London, falling steadily all night with the inevitable power of the will of God. Everything became simple and white. All straight edges were gently rounded, all corners blurred and softened.

As it snowed, Cadbury slept. If she dreamed, she had no recollection of her dream when she awoke. If she failed to dream, then perhaps her waking life was all a dream. But it seemed to her that she had slept for only a short time when she heard the telephone. As she dragged herself upright in bed, she already knew who it would be.

Good morning, Loyola, she said.